God, she was beautiful.

And he hadn't even had that much wine to drink, so this irrational urge he suddenly felt to kiss Laurel could only be blamed on…what? Nature, he supposed.

"What's wrong?" she asked suddenly, taking a step back.

"Nothing." Charles frowned, trying to collect his thoughts and gather them here in the present. "Nothing at all. Why?"

"The way you were looking at me," she said. "It was…" Her voice trailed off and instead her cheeks went pink. "Nothing."

This was dangerous territory. He was on the verge of kissing this woman, when not long ago he'd been ready to fire her and never see her again.

It was crazy.

Elizabeth Harbison grew up in Potomac, Maryland. In 1988, after studying Art History and Theatre at the University of London for a year, she got a BA in English from the University of Maryland. She went on to work as a private chef in the DC metropolitan area. In 1994, Elizabeth turned her hand to writing romantic fiction. Her first manuscript placed second in the sixth annual Harlequin Temptation 'Voices of Tomorrow...Today' contest. A GROOM FOR MAGGIE was published by Mills & Boon® Romance. NYT bestselling author Nora Roberts was quoted on the cover, saying: 'A charming new guide takes you on a delightful trip through the tangled path of true love.' Elizabeth's second romance novel, WIFE WITHOUT A PAST, was a finalist in the Romance Writers of America RITA® contest. Elizabeth currently lives in Germantown, Maryland, with her musician husband and two children.

IN HER BOSS'S ARMS

BY

ELIZABETH HARBISON

All the characters in this book have no existence outside the imagination of the author, and have no relation whatsoever to anyone bearing the same name or names. They are not even distantly inspired by any individual known or unknown to the author, and all the incidents are pure invention.

First published in Great Britain 2006
Harlequin Mills & Boon Limited,
Eton House, 18-24 Paradise Road, Richmond, Surrey TW9 1SR

ISBN-13: 978 0 263 19275 9
ISBN-10: 0 263 19275 X

by Antony Rowe Ltd, Chippenham, Wiltshire

IN HER BOSS'S ARMS

To my extraordinary editor, Susan Litman, who has offered great ideas and great support, and always—*always*—done it all with great finesse, intelligence, and—thank goodness—humour.

Here's to you, Susan.

PROLOGUE

Twenty-five years ago

"WE CAN ONLY AFFORD TO adopt one child," the mother said firmly. "I know she has two sisters, but we just...we can't afford to take proper care of three."

Virginia Porter, director of the Barrie Home for Children in Brooklyn, looked at the young couple who wanted to adopt the toddler who had come identified, by a bracelet, only as "Laurel." They were a nice couple, there was no doubt about it. The background check hadn't revealed anything of concern, and Virginia knew that parents who could afford to take good care of one child might still be stretched thin by taking on three.

Still, it broke Virginia's heart to watch the three girls playing together, unaware that one of them was about to leave forever.

"Please understand," Pamela Standish went on. "It's not that we don't like the other two girls. We could have taken any of them, but we feel the brunette looks most like us and we hope that will help her feel like she's one of us."

"Honey, maybe we could think about it," the husband interjected softly.

"We can't," his wife responded, her voice a bit too hard for Virginia's tastes. She turned back to Virginia. "And we'd like the file closed until she's eighteen. While we do intend to tell her she's adopted, I don't want anyone else getting into her records before she's of age."

Virginia exchanged glances with Sister Gladys, the tender-hearted nun who helped her care for the children. "There are laws protecting her from that," she told the woman.

"But I've written her a note," Sister Gladys said. "About her time here, and her sisters."

"I don't want her to know about them," Pamela Standish said. "It will only make her feel like she's missed out on something."

"But she must know," Sister Gladys said. "Someday she'll want to know her sisters."

"Hush, Sister Gladys," Virginia said, noting the

alarm on the Standishs' faces. "It's up to them. You know that."

The discussion was interrupted by a small voice. The blonde-haired child, Lily, was wobbling toward her sister.

"Lor," she said, determinedly making her way over the field of toys. Lily was the headstrong one. She never let anything get in the way of what she wanted.

Pamela Standish put a protective arm around Laurel, as if she was afraid little Lily would come take her away.

"Hi, Lor," Lily said, smiling big. She put her arms around Laurel. "I 'ov you, Lor. Don't go, 'K? Don't go. Don't go."

Sister Gladys began to cry.

CHAPTER ONE

A COLD WIND WOOSHED ACROSS the Hudson River Valley, slicing through Laurel Midland's thin knit coat and sending leaves swirling around the black wrought iron gates outside the Manor House of Gray Manor Vineyards.

Behind the house stretched acres and acres of the vineyard, as far as the eye could see, making the house seem even more isolated.

Laurel glanced uncertainly at the taxi cab that was already trundling away down the empty winding road, and felt her nerves tingle.

She'd never actually worked as a nanny, but she'd taken the position with confidence, knowing it was just the sort of thing she could do and do well.

But looking at the house before her, she wondered if there had been some kind of mistake. The place looked like a mausoleum. It was hard to imagine *anyone* living in there, much less a six-year-old child.

Certainly there was no evidence on the grounds of a child being present—no bike, no colorful plastic toys, no favorite doll with chopped hair, accidentally left behind in the garden…

Nothing.

For a moment, Laurel considered turning and leaving, but leaving wasn't really an option. She needed the money and, honestly, she craved the protection that a fortress like Gray Manor looked like it could provide. She would have to get over her apprehensions, that was all there was to it.

Besides, caring for one little girl was a lot easier than the work she'd been doing these past three years with ill children in Eastern Europe, helping get them vaccines and teaching them English. This job would provide the perfect segue between the hell she'd been through and the life she was determined to create for her future.

A quiet life, somewhere upstate perhaps, teaching school.

A *normal* life.

Would she ever have that? Given her past, it didn't feel like it was even possible.

And given her present…well, the very idea

seemed ludicrous. She'd gotten herself into a situation that could never, ever be normal.

Could she ever find her way out of it?

The wind lifted again and Laurel shuddered with the cold. Never before had she felt quite so alone. She didn't like to give in to fear, but there was something so ominous in the wind, as if it were whispering a warning for her to run away while she still could.

But Laurel had never run away from a commitment and she wasn't about to start now, no matter how compelling her fear was. Like most emotions, it was an illusion. A lie.

One of many lies in her life now.

She raised her hand and pressed firmly on the gate buzzer.

There was a hiss and a crackle from the little speaker, then a voice asked, "Yes? Who is it?"

"Laurel Midland."

Silence followed.

Laurel added, uncertainly, "The...the new nanny."

"Oh! Yes. Hold on." The speaker went off with a pop and there was a long moment before the gate clicked and slowly opened, like the robed arms of doom ushering her in.

Laurel shook her head at her own imagination and readjusted her grip on the small, tattered leather suitcase that held all of her worldly possessions: her clothes, passport and personal papers, and the tiny i.d. bracelet she'd worn as a baby in the hospital. With one deep, steadying breath, she made her way up the driveway to the door.

She lifted her arm to knock, but it opened before she could make contact, and a short, wide woman with cottony white hair piled atop her head, and a pale blue dress cinched around her generous girth, smiled and said, "Miss Midland, we're *so* happy you've arrived. I'm Myra Daniels, the housekeeper, have been for forty years, do come in, dear, don't just stand there in the cold." She took Laurel's suitcase from her, and ushered her in, continuing to chatter as she led her into a beautiful marble foyer. "Welcome," she said, setting the case down by the foot of a grand staircase, "to Gray Manor."

"Thank you," Laurel responded, and she had to admit that so far her reception was far warmer than she'd expected.

"Your charge will be Penny. She is six years old and has had a rough time of it in her life already. Her parents were in a car accident in Italy a year and a half ago, and her mother, Angelina, was killed."

Laurel's heart constricted with sympathy for the child she had yet to meet. "Oh, I'm so sorry!"

Myra Daniels gave a tight nod. "It was tragic for the child. As a result, her father has floundered a bit in finding the right caretaker for her. He has his ideas about what sort of person it should be, but he's wrong."

Laurel noticed she didn't say that the father was also grieving the loss of his wife, but she knew better than to ask about that. "What sort of person does he think it should be?"

Myra waved the question away. "Never you mind. You will be perfect, I can tell already. Now Miles will take your bags to your room. *Miles!*" She turned her head fractionally to the side, and repeated, "*Miles!*"

"I'm coming, I'm coming." A tall, narrow, hunched man shuffled down the hall, his posture an almost perfect question mark. The top of his head was bald, and gleamed under the light of the wall sconces. "Don't need to keep bellowing for me." He looked up and when he saw Laurel his expression eased. "Oh, hello. Are you the nanny?"

"Yes, I am." She extended her hand to him. "Laurel Midland."

"Miles Kerry." He smiled, revealing a mouthful of crooked teeth.

"You're very young."

That took her aback. "Not *that* young."

"Have you met Mr. Gray yet?"

"Not yet," Myra Daniels snapped, shooting him a silencing glance. "You just take her things on up to her quarters while I take a moment to show her around."

"That won't be necessary," a voice boomed from behind. "She won't be staying."

Startled, Laurel turned to see a broad-shouldered Adonis of a man coming toward them. He wore casual business clothes but somehow on him they looked formal. In fact, his entire demeanor seemed formal and stiff.

"This is Mr. Gray," Myra said, taking Laurel by the arm and leading her to the man so he wouldn't have to navigate so much space on his own. "Charles, this is Laurel Midland, Penny's new nanny."

He gave the housekeeper an impatient look, then turned his piercing green gaze on Laurel. His face was pleasant enough apart from those eyes; a straight, unremarkable nose; nice curve of the mouth; solid, masculine jaw, and a thatch of sandy brown hair that gave him the appearance of a boy who had been at play all day.

But those eyes, shrewd and cool, defined his whole appearance. His eyes were the eyes of a man who had seen too much and doubted most of it.

"I thought I made myself clear on that matter," he said to the housekeeper.

"Quite," Myra Daniels said to him. "Now, aren't you going to greet Ms. Midland?"

An awkward moment shivered through the room.

Laurel decided to take the bull by the horns. "I'm very pleased to meet you," she said to him, smiling and holding out her hand. She figured it was better to approach this without preconception. It would have been foolish of her to be intimidated by his looks.

But when he only looked at her hand without taking it, she drew it back. "I'm very happy to be here," she said, the sentiment landing with a dull thud on the highly polished floor.

Charles looked her over. "Is that so."

"Yes…" What could she say? He was her employer. Obviously she had to tread lightly and follow his cues. "And I'm excited to meet Penny. We're going to have a great time together, I'm sure."

"A great time," he repeated, then glanced at Myra before looking back at Laurel and inquiring, "Is that the job of a nanny, do you think? To provide a great time?"

Laurel wasn't sure what the *right* answer to that question was, or what answer he wanted, but she knew her own thoughts on the matter and decided it was best to just be honest. "I think that's a very large part of the job," she said, nodding.

He looked at Mrs. Daniels again. "You see the problem."

"I'm sorry?" Laurel asked.

He didn't look back at her, but instead said, to Myra Daniels, "My priority is not my daughter's recreation but her education, as you are well aware."

Laurel suddenly felt like she was eavesdropping on an argument she didn't want anything to do with.

"Charles, you need to give this a chance."

"I'm sorry," Laurel said. "But is there something I can do to alleviate your concerns, Mr. Gray?"

He turned his gaze back to her. "I don't think you can, no."

She felt the job slipping through her fingers like wet, gloppy sand. "I realize it's difficult to entrust your child into someone else's care, but I assure you she and I will get along wonderfully. You have nothing to worry about."

A small, ironic smile touched the corner of his mouth. "That's optimistic."

"In this line of work, I think it's best to be optimistic." The truth was she *had* to be optimistic. Otherwise, given the sorry state of her life, she'd have trouble finding a reason to wake up in the morning.

"I would imagine that it might serve you well to be *realistic*," Charles Gray countered. "In *any* line of work."

She shrugged. "Maybe. But it serves *Penny* better for me to be *optimistic*."

He appeared to be holding back either a smile or a growl, she couldn't be sure which. "And who is served by you being argumentative?"

She smiled. "I prefer the term *persistent*." She raised an eyebrow. "Persistence pays off for everyone."

He nodded thoughtfully. "Miss—"

"Midland."

"Miss Midland, you seem like a nice girl."

She bristled at his use of the word *girl* but stood her ground and fixed a smile on her face in response to what he surely thought was a compliment and not condescension. "Thank you."

He continued without acknowledging her thanks. "So what I'm saying may seem a bit harsh." He frowned. "My apologies up front for that."

Uneasiness swept over Laurel like the cold wind that pressed against the window panes. "I…don't understand."

Miles, who was standing by, let out a long breath and when Laurel glanced at him, he flashed her the wide-eyed look of a teenager who was glad *he* wasn't the one in trouble this time.

Myra Daniels shot him a look.

Clearly Charles Gray had at least *some* of the people around him completely cowed.

Laurel was determined that she wouldn't be one of them. "What is it you're getting at, Mr. Gray?"

"Ah, direct." He smiled and it transformed his face. He went from ordinary, even a little menacing, to achingly attractive. The white, even teeth of the football captain; faint laugh lines around his light green eyes; dents that weren't quite dimples etched into his fading-tanned complexion. "I like that."

Laurel's heart tripped, and she reminded herself that it was from the surprise of his smile, not the attractiveness of it. "Good. I'm getting the impression you're the same way."

"Absolutely."

"Then we should get along just fine, don't you think?" She wasn't truly getting that impression at all, but she had dealt with difficult people before and she was pretty sure she had Charles Gray's number.

Men like him would take even a slight sign of weakness or uncertainty and turn it into a battleground.

And while Laurel had her share of uncertainty—

especially about this job—she needed the work far too much to let it slip away if there was even a chance it could work out. Her widowed father was no longer able to work, and he was having too much trouble meeting the house payments with his social security check, especially during the cold winters upstate when the oil was so expensive.

Laurel had never been particularly close to her father—he'd been kind, but had deferred to her late mother. Her mother had been a jealous and domineering woman who had waited until Laurel was sixteen to tell her she was adopted, and had then made a huge point of explaining that *she* had wanted Laurel and that Laurel's biological parents had *not.* It wasn't easy for Laurel to live with such a woman, and she thought it might have been even harder for her father.

So now that he was alone, she wished him peace, and the ability to live out his life in the home he'd built. With the money she'd earn with this job, she could take care of his modest financial commitments. This job not only represented a new job for her, but it was also a comfortable end for her father.

"Oh, I think I can confidently predict that our entire relationship will be characterized by honesty and directness," Charles Gray answered.

Miles coughed, and his shoes squeaked on the marble floor as he gave a quick, quiet nod and shuffled quickly away.

Myra watched him go with narrowed eyes.

Laurel tried for a moment to read the older woman's expression, but all she got was an encouraging smile and the slightest of nods.

She returned her attention to Charles Gray. "I'm glad," she said. "It sounds like we're off to a good start."

"You could put it that way." He gave a quick nod, then looked at Myra. "I assume you'll take care of severance and so on?"

Laurel was puzzled for a moment by his mention of severance, but then realized he was asking the housekeeper to take care of ironing out any lingering details of Laurel's contract.

And it didn't appear Myra wanted to do it.

"Mr. Gray, I wish you'd reconsider," the woman answered him, fastening her watery blue eyes on him.

"I know you do, Myra."

Laurel swallowed and made an effort to stand her ground, fighting a childish impulse to wail *what's going on? Please just give me the job!*

"Give it a chance this time." Myra's expression

was intense as she looked at him. "Please. For Penny's sake."

Mention of the child tightened his expression and drew his mouth into a hard line. "It's Penny I'm thinking of."

"I'm NOT sure you know what she needs. Penny needs a youthful, energetic caregiver. Someone who can bring a little life back into this house—"

"I *know* what my daughter needs," Charles barked, his voice echoing through the room like that of the beast in fairy tales.

Myra stood her ground. "I believe Ms. Midland fits the bill."

Laurel shifted uncomfortably. She'd taken the job in order to work as a nanny, not to change the tone of an entire household. She wasn't sure she wanted to take on whatever huge task it was Myra had in mind for her.

Charles Gray gave the housekeeper a long, hard look, then said, "Please write the check for Ms. Midland."

"Check?" Laurel asked him, knowing in the pit of her stomach that she'd lost the battle. But one thing she'd found in her life was that sometimes battles could be turned around by the sheer audacity of pretending one didn't know one had lost. “Our agreement was that I’d be paid at the end of every week.”

“Or at the end of your service,” Charles Gray said, with a single nod. “Which is now.”

“Wait,” Laurel said, stopping him as he turned away from her.

He raised an eyebrow.

Stall, she thought madly. *Change his mind.* “Are you saying you want me to leave?”

He nodded. “That’s right.”

“But my job—you only just hired me!”

“I’m sorry.” He gave a small shrug that said he wasn’t really sorry at all. “But you’re fired.”

CHAPTER TWO

"FIRED?" LAUREL REPEATED incredulously. "You're *firing* me before I even start to work?" It was such an ugly word. She'd never been fired from a job in her life.

And this was definitely no time to start.

"Your services aren't needed here." His voice was dismissive, cold. Like he'd done this a thousand times and had long since lost any sympathy for the recipient of the bad news.

"But how is that possible? They were needed enough to hire me just a couple of weeks ago."

"That's debatable." He gave Myra a significant look.

"Look, I know you want someone else, a different kind of person, but with all due respect I didn't see a line of applicants lined up Mary Poppins style on your front porch."

"Interviews are by appointment."

"Actually, she has a point," Myra interjected, a sly look on her face. "We don't have any other interviews set up and we *do* need someone to begin right away."

They were interrupted by the sound of light footsteps tripping down the hallway into the foyer.

Laurel looked and saw a small girl with long chestnut hair and a dress that looked just a little too small for her, coming toward them. Her head was down and she was humming an aimless tune and fussing with the blonde hair of a porcelain doll.

At the instant she looked up, Laurel noticed the child's face went white with surprise. She started to turn and run away, but Laurel called out to her. "Hello!"

Myra followed her gaze and said, "Penny, come on back here."

The child slowed and turned with obvious reluctance.

Mrs. Daniels smiled at her. "Come on, dear. It's all right."

"Let the child be," Charles interjected. "There's no point. Why confuse things?"

"This is Miss Laurel," Myra said, extending a hand to the child to usher her forward.

"Myra," Charles said in a warning tone.

Laurel wasn't sure what to say, given that Charles Gray had just told her he didn't need her services. But she did know that she couldn't ignore the child, regardless of whether her father was going to hire her or not. "Hi, Penny," she said, squatting down to the girl's level. "That's a pretty doll. What's her name?"

Penny said nothing, and she didn't meet Laurel's eyes.

Laurel could feel Charles looking at Myra, probably with a *see? I told you!* expression on his face.

Laurel pointed to the name embroidered on the front of the doll's old-fashioned pinafore dress. "Marigold?"

The child nodded.

"That's a pretty name. It goes perfectly with her gold hair."

Penny looked at the floor.

"Marigold has a new dress," Myra said, keeping the conversation going.

Behind Laurel, Charles made a noise of impatience, or perhaps disapproval.

"Oh, can I see?" Laurel touched the doll, and, with the smallest movement, Penny relinquished the doll.

It was indeed a beautiful porcelain doll, with pale bisque skin, periwinkle blue eyes and a small bloom of pink in her cheeks. It looked like an antique, but the crisp green pinafore dress Penny had put on it was still creased from the package it had come in.

"Oh, she's really wonderful." Laurel tried to look at the doll more closely, but Penny kept a grip on the arm.

"Don't you want me to see her?" Laurel asked.

Penny shook her head, and pulled the doll back. Her eyes were filling with tears.

Was she…was she actually *afraid* of Laurel?

Laurel backed off, not wishing to scare the child. "I hope I get to see her later," she said. "But you don't have to show her to me now if you don't want to."

She thought it was over, that the child was going to run away from her and Charles was going to lower the final boom on her hopes of having a job, but, to Laurel's surprise, Penny hesitated for a moment, then spoke.

"She's sick." Her voice was pitifully small. "Her arm's broken." She took her hand away and showed Laurel a large chip of Marigold's porcelain arm.

"Oh, no."

"Are you a nurse?"

"Well…"

"Can you make her better?"

It was a clean break, all it would take would be a

little glue to make a pretty good patch job. It looked as if that had been done on her leg once already.

Laurel glanced at Charles Gray, who was scowling, though not necessarily *at* her so much as at the situation. For whatever reason he obviously didn't want Laurel working for him.

Myra came toward Laurel and Penny. "Why don't you two go on up to Penny's room for a moment and see if you can get Marigold patched up." She gave Laurel a pleading look and said, under her breath, "Let me speak with him for a moment."

"*Can* you fix her?" Penny asked again.

"I think I can," Laurel said. "Do you have any glue?"

The child nodded. "It's in my room."

"Show her," Myra urged.

The child glanced at her, then at Laurel, then at the stairway. The one person she didn't look at was her father.

Myra gave Laurel a nod.

So Laurel went with the child, nervous at the thought of what might transpire between Myra and Mr. Gray. Or, more to the point, what they'd say to Laurel when she returned.

Laurel followed Penny up the staircase and down an impossibly long hall, lit every few feet by ornate sconces. Penny stopped at the last door on the left and opened it to reveal a high-ceilinged, gilded room, far more suited to a dowager duchess than a six-year-old child.

She walked purposefully across the floor, her small footsteps clopping on the cold marble floor, her back ramrod straight. She stopped at a small desk, and lifted the top of it. Laurel could see that the contents were neatly arranged. The child took a bottle of glue out and brought it to Laurel. "Is this the right kind?"

Laurel looked at it. A brand new bottle of school glue, it looked like it had never been used. "Let's give it a try." She glued the parts together, then handed the doll to Penny, saying, "If you hold onto it like this for a few minutes, it will probably stay well enough for you to set her down. In a few hours it'll be completely dry and she'll be as good as new."

For the first time, the child smiled and Laurel saw a small shadow of her father's face. "Thank you," she said quietly, looking down admiringly at the repair. "You're a good nurse."

I'm afraid your father doesn't think so, Laurel thought, but she didn't say it. Instead she said, "Thank you."

"You're not going to stay and be my nanny, are

you?" Penny asked, looking up at Laurel and meeting her eyes.

Laurel shrugged. "I honestly don't know."

"No one does."

That was odd. And more than a little ominous.

"I'd *like* to."

Penny's face settled into a stillness almost mask-like. She turned away from Laurel and carried the doll with her to look out the window. "It's getting cloudy out. Maybe it will snow."

Laurel wanted to reach out to the girl, but she knew it wasn't her place. "Maybe it will," she said. "Well, I'd better get back downstairs now." She went to Penny and laid a hand lightly on her shoulder. "It was fun meeting you. And Marigold."

"Do you like me?" Penny asked.

"Of course." Laurel was so surprised by the question that her vehemence came out sounding like anger. She knelt down. "Yes, I really do."

Penny pulled the doll closer and Laurel was glad to see the chipped arm didn't move. "And Marigold too?"

"Very much." Laurel smiled.

Penny's expression softened slightly but it would be an exaggeration to say she smiled. "I wish you could stay."

"Me too." Impulsively, she gave the child a kiss on the cheek before leaving the room and making her way back through the cavernous halls to the stairway.

When she got down, Charles Gray and Myra Daniels were no longer in the foyer where she'd left them and for a moment she felt a feeling like panic, wondering what she was supposed to do now. Then Myra came hurrying through the parlor toward her. "Mr. Gray is in his office waiting for you," she said, a little breathless. "It's right this way."

"Mrs. Daniels, I don't understand what happened," Laurel said. "Why did he hire me if he didn't want a nanny? Or was it something about me, personally, he didn't like once we met?"

"Oh, no, no, no, nothing like that," Myra reassured her, with a pat on the arm. "Truthfully, I was the one who contacted the agency and I didn't ask for what he wanted."

"Which was…?"

"Someone…older. Stern." She shook her head. "He did not want a beautiful young woman like you in the house."

Laurel felt her cheeks go warm. "I'm not beautiful."

"He thinks you are."

Her cheeks got hot but before she could go so far

as to feel flattered, Myra added, "And he doesn't like that."

"I'm afraid I really don't understand."

Myra gave a light chuckle and she led Laurel down the hall. "I apologize for that. I'm sure it seems like I'm talking crazy nonsense, but the fact is, Charles would prefer to be alone, but if he has to have help in the house, and he does, he wants it to be staid old fogies like me. He doesn't want anyone young and vibrant around because it reminds him that he should be living a little more himself."

"Wow." Laurel wasn't sure how to respond to that. "You seem to know him pretty well."

"I've known Charles since he was a baby, in fact I've known him since *before* he was born. I've worked here for nearly fifty years now, and he has always been the most stubborn person I've ever known. He never reaches out for help, no matter how badly he needs it. It's broken my heart watching him and that child struggle." She stopped in front of a closed oak door. "I know you can help them both, and if you're willing to persevere, even in the face of his resistance, I just know this will work. But you have to be strong. Do you think you're up to the task?"

"I'm up to anything," Laurel said. "Except staying where I'm truly not wanted."

Myra nodded quickly. "I understand that. He'll warm to you when he sees how good you are for Penny, I'm sure of it. If he sincerely wanted you gone, you would be miles away by now."

From what little Laurel knew of Charles Gray, she could believe it. "So he's there?" She indicated the door.

"Yes." Myra gave a quick knock on the door, then opened it. "Miss Midland is back."

"Come in," Charles said heavily. His shifted his gaze to Myra. "I'll speak with her alone."

"Very well." Myra gave him a nod, then winked at Laurel and left the two of them alone.

"You've gathered, no doubt, that my housekeeper is a very pushy woman." The words may have been harsh, but he said them with affection. "If I don't let you stay, I will never hear the end of it."

"I'm not sure that's a good reason for me to be here," Laurel ventured. Lord knew she didn't want to give up the job, but she also didn't want to stay where she was unwelcome.

"Maybe not, but it's my reason for asking you to stay. Just temporarily." He gave a shrug. "So that I can finally shake her meddling. Or at least try."

"Temporarily?"

He nodded. "Here's what I propose. One month.

I'll pay you for the entire term of your contract, which I believe was six months. At the end of this month, you'll move on. I don't care what excuse you give. Sick dog, marriage proposal, whatever." He raised an eyebrow over one clear green eye, making him appear even more shrewd. "I do assure you that you will leave with the cash in your pocket."

It was more than she could have hoped for, under the circumstances, and though she wanted to object on behalf of Penny's well-being, it was not for herself that she was earning this money so much as for her father. It would be unconscionable for her to stand on pride at this point and risk his home when there was the possibility that she could use the time to make Charles Gray see she was good for Penny after all.

"I accept your terms," she said to him, "though I have to tell you that I intend to prove to you that I'm good for Penny."

He gave a half-shrug. "And I think she needs someone more mature to take care of her, especially since I spend a great deal of time away on business. But having you here to get her ready for school and take care of her before and afterwards gives me the time I need in order to find someone new."

Or someone old, as the case may be. Laurel hated

to accept this but there was nothing more she could say. From now on it was her actions that would speak for her. “Fine.” She nodded.

“There’s just one more thing,” he added ominously. It was as if the light shifted, and shadows crossed his face.

“What’s that?”

“You need to stay out of my way. I want to be left alone.”

“But—”

“I realize Mrs. Daniels hired you, not only for Penny, but with an eye toward,” he shrugged, and finished with what must have been a quote from Mrs. Daniels herself, “bringing *me* back to life.”

Laurel cocked her head and looked at him. “You appear to be quite alive to me,” she said sharply.

He lifted his eyebrows. “I didn’t mean it literally.”

“Neither did I.”

He looked at her for one chilly moment, then said, “You’re not a difficult sort, are you?” There was an edge to his voice that might have been humor but she couldn’t read him well enough to be sure.

Still, she smiled. “Not at all.”

“Hmm.” His look was skeptical.

Why it sent a shudder through her, Laurel couldn’t say. But it wasn’t an altogether unpleasant feeling.

"Tell me something, Miss Midland."

"Yes?"

"Why are you willing to stay under these admittedly unusual circumstances?"

She cleared her throat, trying to buy time. She didn't know this man and she didn't want to give him personal explanations that she knew were not really any of his business, yet she didn't want to be impertinent and tell him it was none of his business. "I need to work to support myself," she said simply. "When I took this job, I had to turn others down." It was a lie, but a small one. Surely *something* else would have come along, even given the poor economy in the town where the agency was located. "I had projected this income into my budget."

He steepled his fingers in front of him. "You sound like a very practical woman."

"I try to be."

"Then let me give you some advice." He leaned forward, and looked her over with piercing eyes. "It's not usually a good idea to count your money before it's in hand."

How dare he condescend to her that way! She raised her chin in defiance and, honestly, some false bravado. "I've found that when I have a written contract, as I do in this case, it's usually fairly safe to plan on the income."

He leaned back again, nodding slowly. "Contracts always have loopholes."

"For both parties."

He looked at her with interest. "True."

She wondered what was really going on inside his head.

There was no way to tell, though, as he said to her, "One month, Miss Midland. And thank you for your cooperation."

CHAPTER THREE

CHARLES KNEW EXACTLY why Myra was so intent upon Laurel Midland staying. It was because, as he'd told Laurel herself, she wanted the girl to infuse some life and youth into the house.

But he suspected that Myra had more in mind than that. He was quickly discovering that Laurel Midland was not in the least bit cowed by Charles, or his power, or his position in society.

She was what Myra Daniels liked to call "spunky."

To him that translated as "difficult." He could tell that much already.

For one thing, Laurel clearly hadn't been around the block enough times to learn her place. Not as a servant, of course, but as an *employee.* It seemed likely that her time in the American Help Corps had actually bolstered her initiative to the point where she didn't take instruction very well.

On the other hand, it was possible that he just wasn't used to having someone around him who expressed independent thoughts.

In a way it was refreshing, but in another way it was completely frustrating.

Especially when it came to raising Penny, since, truth be told, he hadn't been that involved in the process while Angelina was alive. Angelina hadn't been what he'd call a *devoted* mother…it was more that she was a good manager, with strict social aspirations. Which had amounted to the same thing, in terms of picking the right school, being involved in school functions, arranging for after school care and programs, and so on.

Angelina had conducted Operation: Child-rearing with the precision of a drill sergeant and, although Charles didn't always feel it was the best way to nurture a new human being, he realized now that Penny was used to that kind of scheduling and predictability.

And over the past year and a half, she had had two different nannies who hadn't worked out. One had left because her daughter had a baby in California and needed help, and the second had left when her boyfriend of ten years had finally proposed and they got married and moved to

Wisconsin. But the thing those two had had in common, both with each other and with Angelina, was that they were strict, no-nonsense care givers. Bedtime was strict, meals were balanced, school was mandatory not optional.

If he hired a nanny now who was a free spirit, a young girl who was going to place emphasis on fun instead of routine, Penny was likely to get confused.

And if Penny *didn't* get confused, but instead flourished under Laurel's care, what would happen when Laurel inevitably moved on? A woman as young, and beautiful, and lively as Laurel wasn't likely to spend her prime years cooped up in an old mausoleum like Gray Manor. And even if that was what *she* intended, some guy would surely come along and snatch her up. Even Charles could see that Laurel Midland had some damned attractive assets.

No, a middle-aged or older woman who'd already married—or decided not to—was more likely to stick around for the twelve years or so it would take to raise Penny into adulthood with consistency.

That last nanny had caught Charles off-guard, but he maintained it was a fluke. His theory in hiring her had been correct, he just hadn't taken the long-time boyfriend into account.

Henceforth he was going to try and ferret out any

of that kind of information first, so as not to make the same mistake again.

He also wasn't going to make the mistake of letting Myra Daniels handle the hiring. He was on to her now.

Myra Daniels was no matchmaker.

And Laurel Midland was *certainly* no match for Charles.

"I know who you really are."

Laurel woke with a start to the words. Had she dreamed them, or were they real? Had she really been found out already?

She turned in her bed to the silhouette of Penny in the dark, standing by her bedside. "Penny?"

The child didn't respond.

Laurel scrambled up and felt for the light by her bed. When she turned it on, it practically blinded her. "Penny? Honey, did you have a nightmare?"

Penny blinked away the light, then looked, bewildered, at Laurel. "What?" She looked frightened.

"Did you come in here because you had a nightmare?" Laurel asked gently, reaching out and putting her hand on the child's shoulder.

"I—I—" Penny looked around, seeming seriously upset. "I don't know. I want to go to my room!"

I know who you really are. She must have been talking in her sleep, just having a dream. It hadn't meant anything.

Maybe it had even been part of Laurel's own restless dreams.

It was probably silly for her to speculate on it so much. Even if Penny *had* said it, she couldn't have meant anything significant by it. They were just the ramblings of a sleepwalking child.

Still…it was disconcerting.

"Penny," she said gently. "Do you remember what you said to me when you came in?"

Penny nodded sleepily. "That I know you're really the fairy princess Rainbow, and that you're magic."

The relief that coursed through Laurel was so intense she had to laugh. All that panic, all that fear, all because Penny had dreamed she was a fairy princess.

She really had to get this paranoia under control.

She missed having a best friend to talk to about this kind of thing. Then again, if she hadn't lost her best friend, she wouldn't be having all of these fears and nightmares at all.

Laurel stood up and took Penny's hand in hers, not bothering to put a robe on over her thin, sleeveless nightgown. She ignored the chill, knowing that it was important that she get Penny back to her own familiar surroundings while there was still a chance she'd fall back to sleep quickly. Otherwise she might be up all night.

She led Penny into her room, which was a couple of doors down the hall, and made her way to the bed by the light of a small night-light plugged into the wall. Marigold was lying on the floor next to the bed and Laurel reached down to get her.

"Looks like someone fell down," she said, tucking the doll into the child's arms.

"I was looking for her," Penny said in her small, tremulous voice. "I thought she left."

"No, no, she just fell out of bed."

"I thought she left," Penny said again, clutching the doll closely to her.

"It's all right, darling." Laurel helped ease the girl into bed, and pulled the sheets up over her. She smoothed Penny's hair back and spoke in quiet tones. "Go on to sleep."

"Go away!" Penny said suddenly.

Laurel was surprised. "What?"

"Go away! I don't want you here!"

This turnaround was so surprising, that Laurel instinctively drew back. "Calm down," she said, trying to disguise the alarm in her voice. "Shhh!"

Penny began to cry. "You're going to go anyway, just go away *now!*"

Laurel hesitated, unsure. She couldn't leave the child in distress, but then again, if she was the cause of the distress, she couldn't very well stay either.

"Shh, honey, it's okay." She touched Penny's head and the child didn't recoil so she stroked her hair some more, soothing her, willing her back to sleep. "I won't go anywhere if you don't want me to."

"They all do."

"Who?" Laurel asked gently. "Who goes?" Had Penny had a string of nannies who had left for some reason? If so, what could that reason be? Were they intimidated by Charles Gray? Afraid of him? "Where do they go?"

Penny didn't answer.

Instead she turned away from Laurel, but soon her breathing grew deep and rhythmic, indicating she'd fallen asleep.

Laurel stood and tiptoed out of the room, closing the door behind her. She stood for a moment in the silent hallway, feeling like her rapid breathing and the pounding of her own heart were loud enough to wake everyone in the house.

There was something creepy about this house. The brooding, mysterious man; the lonely child;

even the nanny with her own secrets to keep…it all felt like a Brontë novel.

And those never had happy endings.

Laurel looked at the clock at the far end of the hall. It was after 3 a.m. and she was wide awake. Her heart was still pounding and her mouth was dry. She decided that, rather than going back to bed and lying in the dark until the sun came up, she'd go downstairs and make a quick cup of tea with the hopes that it would soothe her back to sleep. Heaven knew she couldn't afford to be exhausted on her first real day on the job. Charles Gray already didn't want her here; the last thing she wanted was to prove him right.

The house was still as she padded softly down the grand staircase. There were small accent lights placed about, casting every room in a warm glow. It was funny how much less daunting the house was on the inside, as opposed to the outside, though she wouldn't go so far as to call it *homey.* There was still no evidence of the child who lived here, outside of her own neat-as-a-pin room.

Laurel was going to have to do something about that. Penny was too shy, too scared, and clearly she was way too lonely. She needed to feel like this house was her *home,* not just a holding cell she'd ended up in.

The kitchen was enormous, stretching far and wide. One entire wall was floor-to-ceiling windows overlooking the long sweep of yard, and the vineyard beyond. The appliances were like something from a restaurant, a huge stainless steel refrigerator, eight burner gas stove, and what seemed like miles of butler pantries, housing crystal, china, and silver.

It was hard for an ordinary peasant like Laurel to figure out how to make one single cup of tea. Or to even *find* the tea.

And a cup that wasn't worth more than a week's salary.

After poking around for a few minutes, she found a cavernous walk-in pantry with canned foods and boxed goods, including, to her surprise, some chamomile tea.

One of the shelves also contained a few stainless steel pots and pans, with a tea kettle on a high shelf.

Perfect.

Laurel reached for the kettle, and almost had her hand on it when she shifted and heard her night-gown rip. Startled, she drew her hand back, acciden-tally knocking the shelf below and sending five or six pots clattering noisily to the floor.

When the noise died down, after what seemed like an eternity, Laurel stood still, listening through the darkness in case anyone was coming. Fortunately, the house was big enough that even a ruckus like that didn't reach very far.

She looked at her gown, which had a fair-sized gash in the front, revealing her midriff; then she looked at the shelf where it had gotten caught. A shiny silver nail stuck out about half an inch, just long enough to catch in the eyelet fabric and hold when she moved.

Darn it, she was going to have to go shopping and get a new one now, though, truth be told, in this big house in upstate New York she really needed something warmer anyway. Flannel, maybe.

She tried to be quiet as she stacked the pots up on the shelf again, then instead of trying for the kettle, she decided to just heat some water in one of the smaller stock pots.

She took it out of the pantry and headed for the sink. Her intention was to put the water on and run upstairs to her room to get her robe while it came to a boil. Granted, there didn't seem to be anyone coming into the kitchen at this hour, but it wasn't as if she lived in the place alone. Someone *could* come along at any moment. She knew that.

So she shouldn't have been surprised when she ran into Charles Gray on her way out of the kitchen.

"What the devil's going on in here?" he

demanded. His expression was as dark and menacing as his tone, and that was bad.

Laurel blanched. "I'm sorry, I….I just came down to get a cup of tea."

"And tea required reconstruction of the kitchen?" he asked, his eyebrow raised.

"No, of course not, I accidentally bumped into some pots and they came crashing down. The sound was a lot worse than the event, honestly. Nothing broke and I put them all back."

He looked her over. "And the tea?"

She gestured toward the kettle on the stove, which was emitting a strange smokey-looking steam instead of the usual—oh no! It was smoke. The water had obviously boiled down to nothing.

Biting her tongue to avoid cursing, she ran to the stove and pulled the kettle off. "The tea's been delayed," she said, hoping he'd see the humor in the situation.

He did not. "Ms. Midland, I knew you were not the ideal choice for Penny's nanny, but are you, in fact, dangerous to have in the house?"

"Not usually, no." Suddenly tea didn't seem like much of a libation. This was a vineyard. What she needed at this point was some wine. Maybe a lot of it.

Charles looked at her evenly. "Then why was there a kettle on fire on the stove?"

"Well, it wasn't actually *on fire,*" she qualified. "The water had just boiled down. While I was here talking to you."

He nodded, clearly unconvinced. "You were in the American Help Corps., weren't you?"

She frowned. What did this have to do with anything? She did not want this man, who was looking for a reason to get rid of her anyway, delving into her AHC experience.

If he found out about…well, it would just be a disaster. She couldn't bear to think about it.

"Yes, I was," she said, as lightly as she could, but there was a tremor in her voice that she, herself, could hear. Hopefully he didn't notice it. She laughed, to disguise it. "And I didn't burn one building down while I was there, I assure you."

He narrowed his eyes slightly. "What exactly *did* you do?"

"I taught English to schoolchildren."

"Did you do that alone?"

No, I had a very close friend who taught with me, she thought, but she could not say. It was just too painful—and too frightening—to remember it, much less to answer questions about it.

"There were several others during the time I was there," she said. "We all had different schedules."

"I can't remember exactly where you said you were," he went on. "Was it Lithuania?"

Why was he so interested in this all of a sudden?

"Lenovia."

He gave a low whistle. "Pretty dangerous place. That's a brutal civil war."

She nodded. "Yes, they needed help. I was glad to go." She made a point of yawning. "Now, if you'll excuse me, I really should get up to bed or else I'll be useless to Penny tomorrow."

He hesitated, then gave a single nod.

"So," she went on, nervous from the tense silence, "Good night. It was…nice talking with you. Sorry about the noise. And the kettle." *And everything else about me that you don't like.*

She turned to leave.

"I hope you understand that my objection to you is not personal," he said to her back.

She couldn't help but give a small laugh as she stopped and turned back to him. "With all due respect, it's hard *not* to take it personally, Mr. Gray."

He thought for a moment, then nodded. The concentration in his face made him, although quite serious, extremely handsome. "You need to understand that I gave Mrs. Daniels explicit orders to go through a service in Manhattan, and to hire someone older than you. Someone," he looked at her, "more experienced."

He certainly had *that* right. She was inexperienced, but not with children. "Penny is a sweet, gentle child. I can tell that already. I honestly don't think you need as strict a disciplinarian as you seem to think. To me, Penny seems like a child who, above all else, needs warmth and love and a feeling of safety."

"She has more security than most children."

"Financially, maybe, but she seems worried that everyone is going to leave her." She was treading on thin ice now. It was difficult to get the information she needed in order to help Penny without going too far into territory that was none of her business. "I understand she lost her mother a couple of years ago."

"A year and a half," he said, then looked down.

The tension swelled in the air between them, and it was as if some negative presence of some sort had just walked into the room and pulled up a chair.

And all at once, Laurel understood that the whole family, not just Penny, was still grieving heavily over the loss. There was probably a void in the household that Penny was picking up on beyond her own considerable grief. An extra feeling of loss and sadness that she felt but couldn't quite identify.

Because it wasn't all hers.

"I'm so sorry," Laurel said carefully. "It must be very hard for you. Please let me help. I'd love to try and give Penny even just a fraction of the feeling of safety and love she's missing. It might help ease the burden on you a bit, so that you can…" She didn't know what to say. *Deal with your own grief?* That was too personal. She'd already stepped over the line; she shouldn't be talking to him about his loss at all. She'd probably touched a nerve.

When he looked back at her, she expected his eyes to be soft, perhaps watery with unshed tears, but instead they were cold.

Hard.

"I've already given you the timeline, Ms. Midland. One month. Less if we're able to find someone to replace you sooner."

She couldn't believe it! Just when she thought she was beginning to understand what was going on in the house, just when she thought maybe she'd be able to really help Penny *and* Charles Gray, he dismissed her out of hand. Just like that.

"But—" she began.

He put up a hand to silence her. "I'm sorry. That's

just the way it's going to be." He raked his gaze over her before turning to leave.

Only then did she remember she'd been standing before him all that time in her thin cotton nightgown.

And nothing else.

CHAPTER FOUR

"LAUREL MIDLAND," CHARLES said into the phone, then spelled both names. "She was in Lenovia for the last two years. I don't know where she was before that, but I want to. I want to know everything I can. There's something off about her story, but I just can't put my finger on it."

"If there's anything to find, I'll find it, Mr. Gray," Brendan Brady said. He was the best private investigator Charles had ever worked with, so he believed him. Brendan was the one who had ferreted out the two spies working in production and giving the secrets to Gray's top shelf sparkling brut to Roma Select wines.

Charles never would have suspected his own cousin was behind it, though, in retrospect, he should have.

That was the thing about paranoia. If you were

wrong it was fairly harmless, but if you were right you needed to know it.

So Charles hung up the phone, confident that Brendan would get to the truth. But for some reason, Charles was still a bit disconcerted. Unable to concentrate on work. And it had a lot to do with the Midland girl, though he couldn't say exactly why.

It wasn't as if she were mean, or *completely* incompetent. She talked a good game, and Penny seemed to like her. The problem was that she was young; she was *bound* to want to move on, sooner rather than later, and Penny had experienced enough loss.

Charles was no expert on parenting, or on child care, and he struggled with his own relationship with his daughter, but one thing he did know was that his daughter had had enough loss. And a beautiful young woman like Laurel Midland, just back in the States after a couple of years in a desperate eastern European country, couldn't possibly be able to promise a long-term commitment to the child. As soon as she was used to being back in the States, she'd undoubtedly find a guy and want to spend time with him instead of a child.

And where would that leave Penny?

An older nanny, as he'd argued to Myra Daniels

repeatedly, who had already sown her wild oats—if she had them—and who had committed to families for ten years or so at a time, well, that was exactly the sort of person Charles was determined to hire. Someone who could take the worry of his daughter's welfare at least a *little bit* off his own shoulders.

Because the truth was, with Angelina handling all of the administrative stuff, Charles had simply been the recipient of his child's stories and smiles—as well as smiling pictures of her when he was away. He hadn't had to deal with…well, *whatever* else a parent of a young child had to deal with. For him it had been icing on the cake.

Then Angelina had insisted on joining Charles at a wine show in Italy in the brutal winter months, despite the fact that he was working almost eighteen hours a day and their relationship had long since disintegrated into something between acquaintance and friendship.

Angelina wanted to visit with friends in Italy, and she wouldn't heed Charles's warning that the Italian wine show was not the time or place, thanks to his schedule and the weather.

So she'd come anyway.

He hadn't known that Angelina would get pouty from some sort of row with one of her friends, and that she'd insist on going to the airport to return to New York despite the bad weather. He'd tried to dissuade her from going—any fool could see it wasn't a good time to drive through the mountains—but she'd insisted, swearing she'd walk the ten miles if he wouldn't drive her.

And that was where he'd made what turned out to be the fatal mistake. He'd believed her, and pictured her walking those winding, narrow roads in her defiance, becoming a clear and obvious hazard to herself and any driver along the road.

So he'd followed her, insisted she get into the car, and tried to get to a safe turnaround so he could take her back to town and talk some sense into her.

But he hadn't made it that far. The roads were slicker than he'd anticipated, and far slicker than the truck driver who'd hit them had anticipated. The accident had occurred in the flash of a mere few seconds, and before he knew it, Angelina was gone, and he was so badly injured the doctors thought he might never walk again.

And Penny…. Penny had lost what seemed like the only small chance she'd ever had at a normal life, with a mother to love and take care of her, so…what could he do?

The only answer was that he could find an older,

experienced nanny who wasn't going to fall in love with someone or be flakey and leave. Someone who was ready to stay for the long haul, to be there for Penny no matter what.

And that was *definitely* not Laurel Midland.

Laurel Midland was Miss America compared to what Charles had in mind. In fact, she was Miss America compared to most women—with her raven hair and those beautiful green eyes…she was hot. No two ways about it.

He was having some trouble getting the image of Laurel in her nightgown out of his head. It wasn't as if it had been indecent or anything. The fabric had been thin, certainly. He could clearly see the suggestion of curves when she moved.

He swallowed hard, recalling it.

Laurel stirred something in him. It was probably just the combination of frustration at arguing with her over and over about how wrong he was about raising Penny; and a normal physical attraction any man was bound to feel when faced with such a beautiful woman.

Which was exactly the problem. She was beautiful, young, desirable, intelligent, and single.

Therefore, he would bet that she was bound to move on by the summer, whether because she met another man, or she already had one that she was trying to get away from.

Given her strange and cryptic reaction to his questions about her American Help Corps service, he guessed it might be the latter. She acted like someone who was running away. It was easy to imagine she was running from a past relationship, one she still had strong feelings about.

What other explanation was there for the way she grew uncomfortable whenever questioned about her recent history?

Whatever it was, it seemed like Laurel Midland had some mission other than taking care of a child. Whether it was healing, hiding, or denying, there was something about her that seemed temporary.

And once she'd worked it out, whatever it was, where would that leave Penny?

No doubt about it, there was no room whatsoever for personal feelings. Charles needed to find someone else—someone more suitable—to work as a nanny.

In the meantime, Laurel was better than nothing.

He'd let her stay until he'd replaced her.

Something about Charles Gray made Laurel *very* uncomfortable.

It was probably his complete and total detachment

from anything and everything he should hold dear—namely Penny—but he struck Laurel as one of the most chilly, closed-off individuals she'd ever met.

And she'd met plenty.

The chiseled good looks, which a lot of women would have fallen for, just made him all the more disconcerting to Laurel. Like a photo from the pages of a magazine, of a movie star or a model wearing a three thousand dollar suit. If he'd had bad skin, or thinning hair, or crooked teeth or *some* obvious imperfection, he might have seemed more…human.

As it was, he intimidated the heck out of her.

But she knew she had to try not to let him do that. She knew what she had to do; she knew what Penny needed in a nanny. She'd come to this job knowing she was fully capable of being a competent caregiver to a child. The children in Lenovia had loved her, after all, and she'd absolutely adored them. So she knew much of how to deal with children before she came.

Now, admittedly, Penny was a hard nut to crack. But it was so obvious to Laurel that she *wanted* love, that she *longed for* someone to break through the ice, that it had come absolutely naturally to Laurel to try and get through to her.

And even though Penny was resistant at the most unexpected times—for example, inviting Laurel into her room, then turning away and being wholly uncommunicative until Laurel left—it was clear that she *wanted* intimacy with others. She *needed* it.

Laurel did too, actually.

The truth was, Laurel had never had a very strong feeling of family when she was growing up. Her mother had been distant, and her father…well, her father had just been tired. That her mother was the one to pass away first was a surprise.

Now her father was alone in that house, doing little apart from watching television. But Laurel still felt strong obligation to do what she could to help him, and that meant keeping her job with Charles and Penny Gray.

CHAPTER FIVE

"I'M HAVING TROUBLE FINDING out anything incriminating about this Laurel Midland," Brendan Brady said to Charles. He sounded disappointed.

Charles wanted to be relieved but he still felt cautious. Something wasn't right about Laurel's story. "What *have* you learned?"

"No family. Her mother died recently of natural causes. No aunts or uncles. She's been in Lenovia for five years, but—"

"Wait, *five?*" Charles could have sworn she'd said she'd been there for two.

"Yup. Five. Before that, she was in college. University of Iowa. Had the usual assortment of boyfriends and friends, but didn't appear to keep up with any of them."

How had her former boyfriends and friends just

let go of a girl like Laurel? It was weird. "What about her contacts in Lenovia?"

"Ah, *that,*" Brendan's voice got tight, "was pretty challenging. Her director, a guy named Peter Lucian, was extremely cautious in talking about her. He cited all kinds of confidentiality stuff."

Well, it wasn't surprising. It would have been more surprising if a former director of the American Help Corps had dished on one of his former workers. "Did you get *anything* out of him?"

"Actually he did let one thing slip, though I don't know how significant it was. Apparently one of her close friends there was killed in an accident. Ms. Midland became so upset that she left immediately."

Now, that was interesting. "Did he say who the other person was?"

"Nope. As a matter of fact, as soon as the subject came up he begged off and said he had to hang up. But I checked the records and learned that the girl was also named Laurel—Laurel Standish."

"You do good work, Brady," Charles said with a smile. "What did you find out about her?"

Brendan Brady chuckled and rattled off the facts on Laurel Standish. "Adopted from the Barrie home at age two and a half. Had two sisters—they were triplets. Grew up upstate and had a series of secretarial jobs after high school before going to Lenovia a couple of years ago with the American Help Corps. Nothing remarkable beyond that. Absolutely nothing."

Charles frowned. "Except that Laurel lost her closest friend in a terrible accident. That could explain why she seems so secretive. She might just be grieving."

"It's a good possibility," Brendan concurred. "But I'll keep poking around nonetheless."

"Do that."

Penny came to Laurel one night a couple of weeks after Laurel began, and told her that she was interested in participating in a Halloween celebration the kids at school were talking about. Laurel thought that was a sign of progress for Penny, who previously hadn't displayed any interest in playing with other children.

"It's called the River Witch festival," Penny said. "It's in Chapo—Chapeep—"

"Chapawpa?" It was the next town over, a bit lower rent, on the Hudson River.

Penny nodded eagerly. "I think that's it."

"Let's look it up," Laurel suggested, taking Penny with her to the computer in the den off

Penny's bedroom. Laurel signed onto the computer, got on the internet and went to a search engine to look up the Chapawpa River Witch Festival.

It was there. A day of pony rides, trick or treating at the quaint little shops in town, and other simple, childlike pleasures. It looked like a wonderful event, the kind of thing Laurel wished she'd had in her childhood, and she was glad that Penny was expressing an interest in joining something like that. Up to now—and, admittedly, Laurel had only been involved with Penny for a couple of weeks, although they were an intense couple of weeks—Penny had been so reserved and alone that Laurel was worried about her.

Penny was also taking awhile to warm up to Laurel. She'd have flashes where she'd ask Laurel to help her with something, but that was just about as far as Penny's interest in Laurel went. Now and then she'd ask what Laurel thought of something, but no sooner had Laurel answered than Penny would retreat again, both literally and figuratively.

So when Penny mentioned the River Witch festival, Laurel was encouraged on her behalf.

"My friend at school told me about it," Penny said, as they looked at the web site together.

"Really? Who?" Laurel asked.

"Maggie," Penny said casually, as if she'd mentioned this friend over and over again, though they both knew she hadn't.

"Oh, Maggie," Laurel said, nodding and pretending to know who that was. "So she's going?"

"Oh, yes, she lives there. She goes every single year and she says it's really *really* fun."

Laurel was so encouraged that Penny had made a friend—a friend she'd actually learned a thing or two about—that she wasn't about to do anything to put the brakes on that enthusiasm. "Well, then, I think we should go."

Penny looked amazed. "You *do?*"

"Sure! Why not?"

Penny looked doubtful. Too doubtful for a child her age. "I'm not sure my father would say okay."

That was silly, Laurel thought. What father wouldn't want his child to go enjoy a local town's Halloween festival? "How about this—I'll go talk to your dad about it, okay?"

"Yes!" Penny cried, and threw her arms around Laurel. "Thank you!"

Laurel was so touched by this that she determined, right there and then, to take Penny to the Chapawpa River Witch Festival come hell or high water.

* * *

"Absolutely not," Charles Gray said, without so much as a waver of doubt that Laurel could wiggle her way into.

They were in the library of the house. He was sitting by the fire, reading the *Wall Street Journal,* and looking like a photo from *GQ Magazine.*

Laurel stood before him, feeling dowdy in her modest clothes, with her comparatively ordinary looks, and complete lack of fashion finesse.

"No?" she repeated, dumbfounded. Again she wondered, what kind of parent *wouldn't* want their child to go to a sweet local Halloween celebration?

"No."

"But..." It was hard to know what to say, since his reaction was so completely unexpected. "Why not?"

Charles leveled those beautiful green eyes on her and she felt a chill wind blow between him and her.

"For one thing, the roads there are very narrow and winding. I don't want you to have an accident."

That was ridiculous. "I've been driving for years."

"You've been out of this country for years too," he pointed out. "Did you drive in Lenovia?"

"No," she admitted.

"There you go. Get used to regular roads, like between here and school, before you venture out onto the treacherous ones."

"I hardly think they're *treacherous.*"

He lifted an eyebrow. "Have you seen them?"

"No, but the state highway commission would close them down, or fix them, if they were death traps." She eyed him, challenging him. "If you're going to say no, you're going to have to come up with a better reason than that."

A small muscle tugged at the corner of his mouth, like he was trying not to smile. "I don't owe you explanations for *any* of my decisions," he said coolly, though there was a warmth deep in his eyes that she hadn't seen before. "But, as it happens, I have another very good reason for not wanting Penny to go." He looked back at his newspaper, clearly planning to keep his reasons to himself.

Well, the heck with that. "What is it?"

He set the paper down and looked at her. "I have security concerns."

That one was out of left field. "*Security* concerns? What on earth do you mean by that?"

"I'm not confident that you could keep Penny safe in an emergency."

That wasn't what she was expecting to hear at all. "Safe from *what?* You do realize that all of the witches, ghosts and goblins will be fake, don't you?" She probably shouldn't have been so cheeky but it came naturally to her, always outstepping prudence. "There are no *real* Halloween dangers, you know."

He gave her an exasperated look, but something about that humanized him a notch or two from the impatience he had displayed before. "Believe it or not, I am aware of the customs of Halloween. As a matter of fact, it's those customs, like dressing up in costume, that makes it even more dangerous for Penny."

"I'm afraid I really don't understand."

He set the newspaper down again, deliberately, and explained through a thin veneer of patience, "I am known around these parts as a somewhat wealthy man—"

A seriously wealthy man, she thought. And it wasn't just around here that people knew him.

"—and that is something that has always had the potential to put my family at risk when they're out in public. An event like the one you're describing would put Penny outdoors in a large crowd, surrounded by people in disguises. Strange or threatening behavior could go unnoticed on a day like that. As a matter of fact, even a cry for help could go unnoticed on a day like that."

Laurel could see where he was going, but she disagreed. "This is a *family* event, though. I'm *positive* it will be a safe environment. And Penny really wants to go. She has a friend who's going and, from what I can tell, Penny hasn't had a lot of luck making friends. This could be a huge breakthrough for her."

"And who is this friend?" Charles asked sternly.

Laurel had never known someone who looked so attractive when he was stern.

"Maggie?"

"Maggie who?"

Laurel shrugged. "I don't know her last name."

"What *do* you know about her?"

Laurel sighed. "Well, that she's, like, *six* and probably not a threat to Penny."

He shot her a look. "What about her family?"

"Her family cares enough about her to send her to the best school, just like you have." The more she thought about it, the more convinced Laurel was that this would be good for Penny, and that even if there was trouble—which Laurel seriously doubted—there would probably be a hundred moms and dads right there to help.

Charles, of course, was as unconvinced as Laurel was convinced. He shook his head. "No. Not this time."

"Oh, Charles, come on!" The words flew from her mouth before she had time to censor herself.

He looked at her in surprise, but if he thought anything of her addressing him by his first name, he didn't say it.

She made note of that. Anything that could put them on slightly more equal footing would help her in her talks with him about Penny's welfare. She had a feeling there would be a lot of them.

The strange thing was that she didn't find him nearly as cold and intimidating as she had at first. In fact, if anything, the more she argued with him, the more she saw in him to like.

"What if you hired security to sort of tag along then," Laurel suggested, although she wasn't crazy about the idea of having big conspicuous thugs following them around. "If they could be subtle then maybe it wouldn't intrude on Penny's day, but you'd still be able to breathe easy."

Charles looked at her as if she'd just suggested he throw Penny into shark-infested waters. "I'm not hiring security so you can deliberately take my daughter into a potentially risky situation. Security is helpful at times, but it's not foolproof."

"But—"

"The answer's no," he said, his voice firm. Then he glanced at the clock on the mantle. "Isn't it time for you to go get Penny from school now?"

Laurel looked at the clock.

He was right, darn it.

"Can we talk about this some more later?" she asked.

"No."

"Maybe after dinner?"

"No."

She couldn't help it, she had to laugh at how definitive he was. "Okay, then. Tomorrow?"

He looked at her, those eyes piercing through her, yet warming something deep in her core as they did. There was no mistaking the small light of humor deep in them. "No."

He was impossible. So why was she finding herself wanting to stay and prolong the conversation?

"I guess I'll stop asking then—"

"Good."

"—but I hope you'll at least *think* about it." She left, knowing there was no way he was going to relent.

Neither was she.

CHAPTER SIX

PENNY HAD AN ABSOLUTELY wonderful time at the River Witch Festival.

The event had been exactly as Laurel had anticipated; lots of families, loads of young children, candy corn, hayrides, pony rides on ponies in fancy gold saddles, crisp cool apples wrapped in creamy caramel…everything Halloween should be in an ideal childhood. It was a Norman Rockwell painting come to life.

Until Laurel noticed the man following them.

At first she hadn't thought anything of it. A lot of the kids wanted to do the same events, so groups of adults were hustling groups of children from one place to the next at the same time.

But when Penny had needed to find a rest room and Laurel had come out to find the same man from the bean bag toss line standing by the picnic benches in front of the bath house, without a child in sight, she'd gotten an uneasy feeling.

Maybe he was just waiting for a child inside, she told herself, as she ushered Penny back to the activities with more haste than she normally would have.

He followed.

Laurel's stomach clenched in a knot. Had they found her? Had they discovered her secret and come all this way to get back at her? But no—Pete and everyone else she'd worked with in the American Help Corps had promised to keep her secret. They were her friends, and she trusted them…well, she trusted them with her life.

Then again, maybe Charles had been right all along, and this was someone with an eye toward ransom.

"Ouch!" Penny cried. "That hurts!"

Laurel looked down and realized her grasp on Penny's hand had tightened. She loosened it but didn't let go. "I'm sorry, honey."

"Did you see something scary?" Penny asked excitedly, looking around.

Yes. "No, no, I was just lost in thought." Laurel put on a smile. "We haven't gone to the moon bounce yet, let's go over there."

The moon bounce was good. Enclosed. Crowded with kids and parents. Safe.

"Yay!" Penny slipped her hand out of Laurel's and took off running toward the moon bounce.

Laurel's heart leapt into her throat. "Wait up, Penny." She jogged a few steps to catch up with the child, and put her hand on Penny's shoulder to slow her down. This time she was careful to keep her touch light, even though panic was growing in her rapidly.

Good lord, what was she going to do?

Granted, it might be her imagination. But she had to be cautious. If she was being followed, they weren't going to stop at just watching her bob for apples.

No, they wanted revenge.

They wanted her dead.

"I'm sorry to bother you in the middle of a meeting, Mr. Gray, but I thought you should know."

"Hold on a minute." Charles put his hand over the receiver and said to the marketing department, "I have to take this call. Go back to the drawing board and come up with something else. Look at the other labels out there. We need to compete for the younger market."

The group left, and Charles returned to Brendan Brady. "What's going on? Have you found something?"

"Not yet."

"Then what the devil are you calling for?" Charles demanded. He'd just interrupted an important meeting about re-designing the labels after fifty years. "I told you to call when you found something out about Ms. Midland."

"One of my men just called and said Ms. Midland and your daughter are in Chapawpa."

"What?"

"After we last spoke, I took it upon myself to put a man on surveillance duty. It can be difficult to find information from overseas, so sometimes just following someone's movements will give a clue as to where to look."

Charles wasn't interested in the details of detective work right now. "You're saying she's in Chapawpa *right now?*"

"Yes, at the…" There was the sound of paper. "Chapawpa River Witch Festival. It's some kind of Halloween—"

"I know what it is. I'm on my way. You have my cell phone number. I want you to stay in touch with your guy and if she makes any movement at all, even if she just walks more than ten yards away, I want to know about it."

"You've got it," Brendan said.

"Thanks," Charles said. "You do good work."

Twenty minutes later, Charles was passing the carved wooden sign that read *Welcome to Chapawpa. If you lived here, you'd be home.*

"And if you don't, you're going to have a hell of a time trying to park," Charles muttered, coming upon what was obviously the festival and a parking lot with a handmade sign that said, *Full, please try Windjammer Street.*

No time for that. He parked illegally, figuring he'd rather pay the fine than waste any more time trying to maneuver through the crowds while his daughter was out there, vulnerable, without proper protection.

He could throttle Laurel Midland.

It certainly seemed a more reasonable impulse than the ones he'd been having earlier, when they'd talked in the library.

Then, he'd found himself baiting her to challenge him; watching for her smile; hoping for the twinkle he sometimes caught in her eye.

Now he had just one thought on his mind: getting to them, and getting them back to Gray Manor.

He flipped his phone open and called Stan. "Okay, where is she right now?"

"Hold on." Brendan talked into what had to be another phone. "Near the what? The *Clown Circus?*"

Charles scanned the scene, looking for something that looked obviously like a "clown circus".

"Oh, okay, by the pony rides." Stan's voice came back on to Charles. "You see the pony rides?"

"Yeah, I—" Just then, a figure broke away from the crowd and his heart flipped.

It was Laurel.

He told himself it was the adrenaline that came with the base instinct of locating one's prey, for lack of a better term, and not the way she filled in her faded blue jeans, or the v-cut of her peach colored tee shirt.

"I see her," he said, flipping the phone shut, and walking in great strides toward Laurel and Penny.

Penny was holding a cotton candy, and her face was dotted with blue from the stuff.

She looked really happy.

For just a second, Charles paused, struck by the sight of his daughter's wide smile.

Then he noticed the expression on Laurel's face. It was unmistakably upset. Nervous.

Had someone said or done something threatening?

"Laurel!" He ran to her, put his arms on her shoulders reflexively.

She sank against him. "I'm so glad you're here," she said, her voice quavering.

Then, as if both realized the strangeness of this interaction at the exact same moment, they both drew back.

"I got a call you were here."

"From who?"

"One of my employees…saw you here. Called me."

The expression on her face, which moments before had gone from panic to relief, now turned to anger. "That guy?" She pointed to a non-descript man of medium build, who, upon seeing her point, stepped back into the shadows.

Some private detective.

"I don't know," Charles said honestly. "Probably."

"What do you mean *probably?* Didn't you just say you hired him?"

"That guy over there has been watching Laurel all day," Penny piped, pulling some cotton candy off and shoving it into her mouth. "He thinks she's pretty," she finished, in a muffled voice. "Don't *you* think she's pretty, Daddy?"

Charles looked from Penny to Laurel.

She *was* pretty.

But she was horribly wrong to have brought Penny here, against his expressed wishes.

"Let's get you cleaned up so we can go, honey," Laurel said to Penny, not waiting for a response from Charles to Penny's question, thank goodness.

"But Daddy didn't—"

"Gotta hurry," Laurel interrupted, not looking back at Charles. "Come on, now."

So she knew he was angry, at least. She had the sense to know she'd done something wrong. She just hadn't had the sense to not do it in the first place.

Charles waited, wondering what he could do, what he could even *say,* in the face of such complete disregard for his instructions.

When they came back, Penny was all cleaned up, and still beaming with joy at the day she'd had.

Laurel, on the other hand, had the nerve to still look irritated about the man who'd been following her.

That took some nerve.

Penny ran ahead of them, like a gleeful puppy, thrilled with her surroundings. Charles was glad, because what he had to say to Laurel wasn't rated G.

"I cannot believe you defied my orders this way," he said, as they walked side-by-side behind Penny.

"Orders?" Laurel repeated quietly.

"Instructions, then." It was so typical of her to wind things up in semantics. "Wishes." Wait a minute, he wasn't going to back off like that. She was his *employee,* for heaven's sake. "Orders."

"I didn't realize I was forbidden to come here."

"You weren't," he said shortly. "You were forbidden to bring my daughter here."

"Oh, all right, I know," she admitted. "You did ask me not to bring Penny here, and you are her father, and you're my boss, and I shouldn't have done it. Except…" She gestured toward Penny. "Look at her. She's so happy. I just knew this would be good for her, and I couldn't seem to make you understand that."

"I understood," he said evenly, "that Penny would enjoy coming to this thing. The problem was, and still *is,* that you don't understand the danger it puts her in to come out in public unprotected."

"Nonsense, I was right next to her the whole time."

He stopped. "When I got here, you looked terrified."

Her face reddened. "That's because…"

"Because what?"

She glanced at Penny who had run ahead. "Penny!" She looked to Charles. "We're both going to lose her in the crowd if we don't keep up with her."

They started walking again.

"Why did you look so agitated when I arrived?"

"Because your lousy detective was following me, that's why. You had me spooked by your stories of all the terrible things that could happen and I guess I just," she shrugged, "my imagination carried me away."

"But you understand it could easily have been someone I *hadn't* employed. Then what would you have done?" He looked at her, watching for her reaction.

She swallowed hard, but didn't look at him. "I probably wouldn't have given it much thought at all," she said, though the tensing of her jaw gave him the impression she was lying. "It's like hearing the house settling after someone's been telling you ghost stories. It doesn't mean there's a ghost there, you're just more in tune to every little thing, and every little thing makes you more jumpy."

"You looked more than jumpy."

She glanced at him, her green eyes fiery. "Well, I wasn't."

"You don't have an ex-boyfriend stalking you or anything, do you?" he went on.

Her face went from pink, to sheet-white. "No! Why would you ask that?"

It was a strong reaction.

A little stronger than he'd expected.

"Just asking." He made a mental note to mention it to Stan. Maybe there *was* a crazy stalker ex out there. In which case, he definitely didn't want Laurel around Penny. "Where's the car you brought?"

"We took the train," Laurel told him.

"The train?" It didn't compute. "I did allow you the use of a car for taking care of Penny."

Laurel nodded. "But you said that you didn't want me driving these winding roads with Penny in the car."

He gave a shout of laughter. "I also told you I didn't want you bringing her to this festival at all."

"I know, but I could see the concern about the roads," Laurel said guilelessly, the unspoken *but the rest seemed like nonsense* hanging in the air between them.

Penny stopped and joined a group of children in line for a gypsy fortune teller.

Laurel looked at Charles. "Believe or not, I truly don't want to put the child in any danger."

"As long as you're the one determining what's dangerous," he supplied.

"Well." She sighed. "I wouldn't say that. But I really disagreed with you about the risks of this festival. And, as you can see, the benefits were considerable."

There was no denying that Penny was having the time of her life. And her life had not been one big party, that was for sure. Ever since the accident, she had been more morose and uncommunicative than ever.

Yet there she was, giggling, shouting, laughing with other children.

Charles couldn't bring that out in Penny himself, so he was glad to see it.

Still. "I told you not to do it."

Laurel nodded. "That's true."

"You can't just disregard my instructions."

She nodded again, but this time she said, "I promise I will make every effort not to in the future."

"Every effort?" he repeated incredulously. "Just don't do what I tell you not to do. It's really very simple."

"Next!" a sharp voice called.

Laurel looked to the side, then back at Charles. "I think it's your turn."

"My turn…?" He followed her gaze to the gypsy. "Oh, no. No, no, no."

"Come along, sir," the gypsy barked. "It's your turn."

CHAPTER SEVEN

"GO, DADDY," PENNY urged. "It's your turn!"

Laurel saw this as the perfect opportunity to get Charles Gray grumbling about something other than the way Laurel had conducted—or, she'd admit, *mis*conducted—herself, so she urged him on. "Go get your fortune told. What fun!"

"I don't want to—"

"Charles!" the woman snapped, drawing the startled attention of both him and Laurel. "Come on, we don't have all day."

Laurel and Charles exchanged a glance.

"Go *on,* Daddy," Penny said, oblivious to his discomfort. "She even knows your name!"

It was interesting to see Charles so completely removed from his comfort zone. He was not the sort of man to go in for psychics and fortune telling. Even though Laurel had only known him for a short period of time, she knew that much about him. He was the definition of practical.

Of course, Laurel would have also said he was the definition of unflappable, but he was clearly uncomfortable as his dignity prevented him from making a scene over this.

"Let me see your hand," the gypsy said to him, taking his hand and immediately setting about examining his palm. "Ah…you have been very lucky. You are a survivor."

Charles looked at her skeptically.

She didn't appear to mind. "But you have not been so lucky in love, eh?" She frowned and closed his hand up, looked at his fingers, then opened it again. "You've never been in love?" She looked at him. "How can this be true?"

Yes, how *could* that be true? He'd been married. The product of his marriage, Penny, was standing not three feet from him.

"But you will be," the gypsy added cryptically.

This had been fun at first, but Laurel didn't want Penny hearing this nonsense about her father and mother not having been in love. True or not, the child didn't need *that* in her head.

Laurel was about to say something—she hadn't yet figured out what—when Charles spoke.

"That's pretty standard fortune-telling fare," he said, sounding good-natured, though the tick in the muscle of his jaw told Laurel he was otherwise. "Don't you have anything more specific?"

The woman met his eyes and smiled, revealing dingy grey teeth. "She is here."

"Who?" he asked.

To Laurel's shock, the woman gestured grandly at her. "*She.* The one in your future." She pointed a gnarled finger to a spot in the center of his palm. "The one you spend your life with."

Charles glanced at Laurel, frowned, and looked back at the gypsy. "Unless you're saying my life ends this afternoon, I don't think you have that right."

A tremor ran through Laurel's chest.

The gypsy laughed. "No, no, I never predict death. Only life. And love. This is the woman of your heart."

Charles gave a laugh.

It was kind of insulting, actually.

"That's my daughter's nanny," he said, as if the whole idea of someone falling in love with a nanny was unheard of. Obviously he wasn't familiar with some of the more famous Brontë novels.

"Really," the gypsy said, unconvinced. "I see her as so much more. She appears quite prominently in your future. You will be together." She looked at Laurel again, and let go of Charles's hand. "Tell me dear, why do you hide who you really are?"

Laurel's stomach squeezed into a knot.

Charles took the opportunity to extricate himself from the woman and instead nudged Laurel in the woman's direction. "Your turn."

He couldn't have known how very much Laurel didn't want to hear this.

She smiled, but didn't manage to make it look natural. It felt more like a grimace. Which it was. "We're going to be late getting back to the house," she said uneasily.

"Nonsense. We've got all the time in the world."

The gypsy reached toward Laurel. "Come. You suffer. I can help. Please."

Laurel looked around. No one except Charles seemed to be paying attention to what was going on with her. The children who had moments earlier been in line behind them had apparently had their attention hijacked by a troupe of spectacularly athletic clowns.

Laurel, never a fan of clowns, would have given anything to join the kids in watching the show.

But she was stuck. She couldn't escape this without appearing either very rude or very guilty of something. Rude she could have handled but she couldn't afford to take the chance of raising Charles's suspicions about any sort of guilt.

So she sat down in front of the woman, very reluctantly.

"You were surrounded by danger. Criminals." She frowned and looked at Laurel. "This was not in this country."

"I was in Eastern Europe," Laurel said. "It was…a politically charged place."

"This was not politics. You were in danger. Someone wanted to get to you."

Laurel tried to swallow the lump in her throat, but she couldn't. Her mouth was dry, and she feared if the woman let go of her hand the telltale shaking would give her away.

She tried to laugh. "Good thing I'm not there anymore."

"But…you are. I do not understand this. You are there and you are here." She shook her head. "It doesn't make sense."

Oh, God. Yes, it did.

It made way too much sense.

Laurel felt Charles move in closer behind her, looking at her palm over her shoulder, as if he could see something there.

"It is okay now," the woman said again. "You may come out of hiding. You and your sisters will finally be happy."

Sisters? Well, at least she'd changed the subject from deception. "I don't have any sisters."

The woman frowned. "You are not speaking to them?"

"No, I don't *have* any sisters. At all." Unless… well, she *was* adopted. It was certainly possible that she'd had sisters or that one of her biological parents had gone on and had more children.

The woman glanced at Laurel's palm again. "You have two sisters. Very, very close to you."

Laurel shook her head. The woman almost had her going, but she *definitely* didn't have siblings that she was "very, very close" to. "Maybe you're mixing my future up with someone else's."

"Not at all."

Laurel drew her hand back and stood up. "Then I don't know how to explain it." No sense in going overboard to explain the possibility versus the probability of biological siblings to a carnival fortune teller.

"You need not explain. Your heart tells you the truth." The woman looked her in the eye with such sincerity in her clear blue eyes that Laurel almost could have believed her. "Now be your own true self. It's important that you stop hiding."

"Who are you really?" Charles asked.

Laurel whipped around to face him. "I'm exactly who I said I was. She's just…" Laurel shrugged, but she was shaking so badly she was afraid he'd hear her teeth knocking together. "It's just nonsense."

"Whoa," Charles said, looking at her oddly. "I was only joking."

"Right," Laurel said, then tried to smile again. "Right. Of course. I knew that. I just wouldn't want anyone else getting the idea that I'm…that this is real." She cast a desperate look at the gypsy.

"Of course," the woman said, with a look in her eye that said she could read Laurel like she was a children's picture book. "It's all just in fun."

"We'd better go," Laurel said to Charles. "It's getting late. Winding roads and all that."

She called to Penny, who was several feet away watching the clowns and together the three of them headed for Charles's parked car.

But Laurel could feel the gypsy's eyes on her back as she walked away.

"Do you think the fortune teller was right?" Penny asked excitedly from the back of Charles's luxury car.

"She definitely wasn't," Charles said quickly, sharply. "She was a fake."

"She didn't *look* like she was faking," Penny said. "And she thinks you two are going to get *married!*"

"The rumor mills will be churning that one up before you know it," Charles muttered.

Laurel looked back into the excited face of Penny. "She was hired to be there, honey. Like the clowns, and the people giving pony rides."

Penny frowned. "Oh."

Laurel didn't tell them it wasn't her first experience with a psychic. She'd spent a long time now trying to *forget* the first psychic she'd seen, back in Lenovia. Everything the wizened old man had said—about her past, what was going on at home, and, as it turned out, about the future—had been exactly right.

Tragedy.

Loss.

Death.

Rebirth.

All of it daunting. All of it true.

Later, Laurel had half-wished she'd maintained her composure long enough to ask the man some questions about her biological parents, but at the time she'd been so freaked out by the experience that she'd hurried away from him as quickly as possible. What the rationale behind that was she couldn't say, except maybe a vague, crazy feeling that if she didn't hear it, it wouldn't be true.

But today's prognosticator…she was different. A carnival gypsy, nothing more. With her crazy talk of sisters, and of Laurel—of *all* people—being the woman Charles Gray would spend the rest of his life with.

It was patently ridiculous.

"Laurel?"

Startled, she turned to face Charles. "Yes?"

"I was saying that fortune telling is just a silly Halloween game, no more real than the tissue paper ghosts hanging from the trees." He gave a slight nod toward the back seat. "Isn't that right?"

"Oh. Yes. Absolutely." She looked at Penny, who looked a little disappointed. "But it was fun, wasn't it? Maybe you could dress up like a gypsy for Halloween night."

Penny brightened immediately. "*Really?* I finally get to go trick-or-treating?"

Oh, no. Laurel didn't need to look at Charles to know that she'd just bungled her way into breaking yet another rule.

"We'll see, honey," Laurel said, grimacing a little. "I'll have to discuss it with your father."

Charles flashed her a dark look. "Actually, there are several things we need to discuss."

"I thought there might be."

"I'm glad to know you're perceptive about *some* things."

"What's persective?" Penny wanted to know.

"Per*cep*tive," Laurel corrected automatically.

"I know, persective, that's what I said." For one amusing moment, Penny wore an expression of impatience that made her look just like her father. "What does it mean?"

"Perceptive means that you *perceive* what someone else means," Laurel glanced at Charles and said pointedly, "even when they're not being clear."

"On the other hand," Charles shot back. "Someone who is *not* perceptive might bulldoze her way through life without any regard to anyone else's feelings or wishes. Even when other people tell her *specifically* how they feel."

"And yet a *perceptive* person might be able to read a situation better than someone who wants what he wants no matter what's best for the people involved." Laurel gave a nod, satisfied with her explanation.

"Sometimes," Charles said, "a person who thinks she's enormously perceptive might in fact be reading things in a way that validates her own philosophies, no matter what the *truth* might be."

"As you can see," Laurel said pointedly, "there are different definitions. But basically it means being sensitive to what's going on around a person." She looked in the back at Penny.

But Penny was looking out the window, her head lolling back against the tawny leather seat.

"Penny?" Laurel said.

"What?" Penny looked at her absolutely innocently.

Laurel had to hold back a laugh. Penny wasn't even listening to them anymore. "Do you understand what it means now?"

"I forgot the word," Penny confessed, then heaved a sigh and looked back out the window. "We passed some horses. Mommy once told me that when you're driving past horses you should wish on the white one."

Laurel felt Charles tense in the driver's seat. "Did you see a white horse?" she asked.

"Yup."

"What did you wish for?"

"Well, actually…" Penny's cheeks went pink.

Laurel sat in dread of what was coming next. No doubt it would be a wish for trick-or-treating, or a party full of gypsies, or something else Charles would wholly disapprove of and blame Laurel for.

"I wished for a horse," Penny finished, with a shrug. "But I don't know how to ride one."

Laurel laughed. "Maybe you should start with a dog."

"You are absolutely determined to cause me the most trouble possible, aren't you?" Charles said, in a voice that would have sounded light to a child, but which Laurel already knew spelled trouble for her later.

"Or a stuffed dog," she added lamely.

Fortunately, Penny seemed to think that was a great idea. Her mouth dropped open and her eyes widened. "I love stuffed animals! Can I get a dog one? Please?"

Catastrophe averted, Laurel told her with confidence, "Absolutely. I'll buy it for you myself."

Satisfied that the problem was solved, she sat back against the soft seat and smiled.

"I need to speak with you tonight," Charles said quietly to her. "As soon as she's gone to sleep."

CHAPTER EIGHT

"I FOUND SOMEONE WHO KNEW Laurel." Rose Tilden Harker said to her sister, Lily, over the phone.

Lily gasped. "Who? Where?"

"Well, actually, her name is Laurel too." Rose glanced down at the notes she'd excitedly scrawled, although she'd already memorized them. "Laurel Midland. Warren's had a guy on the case for us and apparently this woman is just back from Eastern Europe, where she worked with Laurel in the American Help Corps."

"Oh…"

"I know." They'd always been able to read each other's thoughts, and most of the time—like now—they were thinking the same thing. It was bittersweet to think about meeting someone who had known the sister Rose and Lily could never know. But at the same time, it was exciting to think they might be able to learn at least something of the sister they hadn't seen since they were toddlers.

"So she knew her well?"

"Their director, who's still over there, said everyone called them The Laurels, and that they were as close as sisters."

"Ironic."

"I know."

"You know," Lily said, "I just found out Conrad and I might go to New York next week for an event for his father's foundation. Why don't I come early and stay with you guys?"

Rose's heart leapt. It had been a year since she and her sister had shared a dive of an apartment in Brooklyn. In one magical year, both their lives had turned around dramatically, Rose's when she met her husband, Manhattan developer Warren Harker; and Lily's, when she met her husband Crown Prince Conrad, of the small Alpine country of Beloria.

Once Lily had moved to Beloria, obviously the women had seen much less of each other. In fact, it had been two months now. After a lifetime of sharing a room, then an apartment, two months seemed like an eternity.

"Can you come now?"

Lily laughed. "I might need to pack first."

"Buy stuff when you get here. Just get on a plane and come now!" Rose was only half-kidding. The more she talked, the more urgent it felt that they get together and find this Laurel Midland.

For some reason, it felt like the timing was urgent.

"Are you okay?" Lily asked, her voice sharp with suspicion. "Rosie, is there something else going on that you need to tell me about?"

"No, it's just..." Tears formed in Rose's eyes and she was immediately a runny mess. She sniffed.

"You're crying." Lily didn't miss a thing when it came to her sister.

"I know," Rose said. "Everything's fine. I don't know what's wrong with me. I'm just overly emotional lately."

"Are you sure there's not something else?" Lily asked, concern sharpening her voice. "Oh, my God, Rose, are you pregnant?"

Why this surprised Rose, she didn't know. Lily had always been able to read her, whether she was in the room or halfway around the world. "I wanted to tell you when you got here!"

"Oh, Rosie, a baby!" Lily sniffled over the line. "How far along are you?"

"Like three days," Rose joked. "I just found out this morning."

"It's so wonderful! Our family is growing more and more by the moment!"

"I hope so," Rose said, turning her thoughts back to the subject at hand. "But hurry up and get here. We'll talk all about everything then. I just have this weird feeling that if we don't find this Laurel Midland right away, she's going to slip away, just like our Laurel did." She sniffed again, unable to stop the tears that were flowing down her cheeks.

"I'm probably being silly," Rose went on, trying to reassure Lily. "We lost Laurel, so now that it seems like we might have at least one small link to her, I'm just afraid of losing that too."

"I'm on my way," Lily said. "I'll call you the minute I get to JFK. In the meantime, take care of yourself and that little baby you're carrying."

CHAPTER NINE

CHARLES NEVER WOULD HAVE taken Laurel to be one who was easily spooked by something as silly as a fortune teller at a Halloween party, so her reaction to the gypsy intrigued him.

Obviously the fortune-telling was a sham. Total nonsense. True, he hadn't been in love with Angelina, Penny's mother…but Angelina, and those in their inner circle, had known that their marriage was a business merger of both families' properties. A convenience. Had Angelina lived, they would undoubtedly have gone their separate ways by now.

Penny had been the result of a brief time of shared passion during the first year and a half or so of their marriage. But Angelina's pregnancy had been a difficult one and by the time Penny had been born and Angelina was sufficiently healed for an intimate relationship, she'd already moved on to another, more promising, love interest.

Neither Charles nor Angelina had experienced much regret about that. The combined vineyards had prospered. Charles and Angelina's relationship was amicable, their fortune had grown exponentially, making them each far more financially secure together than they had been alone.

But for the gypsy to have said that was nothing more than a coincidence. The kind of romantic prattle that people usually wanted to hear from people like her. Likewise the nonsense about Laurel Midland being prominent in his future. Within a few weeks, she would have moved on and Penny would have a new nanny.

As a matter of fact, he began interviewing them the next morning.

The first was a woman of about sixty-five, with a British accent and stern, but competent, look.

But things didn't get off to a great start. "I have to tell you, Mr. Gray, I do not approve of imbibing alcohol."

"Excellent, I prefer my daughter's nanny be sober."

"As I prefer my employer," she said with an arched brow. "I have reservations about the fact that you are in the business of creating wine."

Well, good. It was probably good for Penny to have a nanny who was strict about such things. Especially as Penny got older. "Don't worry," he said. "It's my business, not my hobby."

She sniffed and gave a single nod of approval. "I'm glad to hear it. I mean no disrespect, understand, but things have to be the way they have to be. No deviation. I am a woman of routine, especially with my charges."

"And what is an example of what your routine might be on a given day?"

She was ready with an answer. "Seven a.m. a breakfast of oatmeal and milk. No juice. It's bad for the teeth. Mid-morning, when she's not in school, we will take our exercise on the grounds. Lunch is at noon sharp…"

She went on and on, showing herself to be completely unyielding to life, and circumstance, and anything else that came along.

Laurel would have hated her, he couldn't help but think. She would have argued for play time, exploration, the freedom for Penny to make her own mistakes and learn from them.

As the day wore on and Charles interviewed one potential nanny after another, he barely had time to come up with his own original conclusions since his head was filled with what he knew Laurel would say. Too stern. Too mean. Too severe-looking. Not loving. Not listening. Not generous.

In short, all of them were Not Laurel.

And he was beginning to see some of the benefits of Laurel's childrearing philosophies, even though he still believed she was too young and pretty to be relied upon to stay.

So what he'd have to do was find someone more like Laurel…to replace Laurel.

It was a little confusing, so he just had to remind himself that he was right and he had to ignore all the crazy little impulses he was beginning to feel about keeping Laurel around.

He called her down to his office later that evening, after she'd put Penny to bed and there wasn't a chance that the child would walk in on them and get upset at the idea of losing her nanny.

Charles was sensitive to the fact that his daughter had lost some pretty important caregivers in her short life, which was exactly why he didn't want Laurel to stay at all when Mrs. Daniels had first hired her, but he needed to do this.

"I know I shouldn't have taken Penny to the River Witch Festival yesterday without your permission," Laurel began as soon as she came in the room. "I just felt so strongly that she needed to be, I don't know, *rewarded* for her willingness to get out and interact with people. She's been such a loner. Mrs. Daniels said she never has friends over and—"

"Hold on," Charles said, stopping her mid-sentence. "Please," he gestured toward the leather chair opposite him. "Have a seat."

She did so, and kept on talking, "Anyway, she's finally starting to make friends at school, and making plans with them for non-school hours is a great sign of her increasing socialization."

He didn't know what to say about that. Socialization wasn't his priority for his child. "She's six years old. Friends, after-school activities, all of that will come with time."

Laurel looked skeptical.

Somehow he knew she would.

"When I was in Lenovia there were children—admittedly, children with hardships Penny doesn't share—but they closed off into themselves. Some of them just *couldn't* be reached. Not with the lack of time and psychological skills all of us had. But we're talking about kids who were just twelve, thirteen years old. They'd lost parents and been shuffled around so much that they didn't trust anyone."

"It's a sad fact that many children lose a parent

or even both parents." Charles was feeling defensive. It was that old guilt popping up again. "It doesn't turn the children into social misfits."

"No," Laurel said, more gently now. Her green eyes softened. "But sometimes when a person gets used to being alone they decide they want to keep on being alone. I'd hate to see that happen to Penny."

"Penny will be fine," he said dismissively. "Actually, I wanted to talk to you about something else."

"Oh?"

He nodded. "While I appreciate your work here, and the way you've embraced Penny so quickly and taken her welfare to heart, I'm afraid we're just going to be sorry a few weeks down the road when she has a new nanny."

Laurel swallowed. "Then how about keeping the nanny you have? I was hoping you'd see how good I can be for her."

He answered carefully. "I certainly see, and appreciate the fact, that you care for her. But I've been clear from the beginning that it's my intention to hire someone more mature. In fact, I began interviewing today."

"Oh." Laurel's expression fell. "Did you find someone you like?"

"Actually, no. But I've got a much clearer idea of what I want." He pushed away the thought that *she* was what he wanted. For Penny, that was. Because it wouldn't work out. "I think we should tell Penny right now that you're going. So she won't get too attached."

"I see." The light that had been in those beautiful green eyes just moments before was gone.

And Charles felt a strange sense of regret about that. He wanted to see her smile again.

He was, as they say, growing accustomed to her face.

Which was as pointless for him as it was for Penny. Maybe even more so, because he had a pretty good idea that Laurel would enter his mind for a long time to come. "I'd like to just buy you out of your contract," he said, though his voice didn't project the definitiveness he'd normally want in a business transaction. "That way you will have ample time to find a new position and you'll be able to support yourself while you look."

"For a couple of weeks," Laurel pointed out.

"Yes."

"That's not worth it."

He was taken aback. "Are you saying you want more money?" he asked, surprised. He would never have taken her for the type who would ask for more.

"No, of course not." She sounded insulted. "This isn't just about the money. It hasn't been since I met Penny."

"Then what do you mean it's not worth it?"

"I mean it's not worth it for me to abandon that child for two weeks' pay."

Charles frowned. "Abandon—what are you talking about? I'm letting you go."

She straightened her back. "And…I suppose I'm refusing."

"Refusing?" he repeated. "You can't refuse to be fired."

"Perhaps not, but we have a contract. It binds you as well as myself. Unless you have good cause—examples of which were clearly outlined in the contract—you cannot dismiss me."

"Not without pay," he explained. "I'm offering to give you full pay for the remaining term of your contract."

"That particular option isn't stated in the contract."

This was unbelievable. "It's certainly implied." Who wanted to stay and work when they were being offered full pay to just *leave?* The girl had to be nuts.

"Implications don't hold up in court, as far as I know," she said, raising her chin defiantly.

Charles was stunned. He'd had to fire plenty of

people in his life. Sometimes he offered them severance packages, sometimes he threatened them with lawsuits. Never had he offered them full pay for the remainder of their contracted term, but he was willing to bet that no one who had ever worked for him would have refused such a generous offer.

Especially if they knew they'd be leaving the job in a couple of weeks anyway.

"I'm not trying to be difficult," Laurel said, as if reading his expression. "I realize, of course, that that's a generous offer. If I were working at a desk job and you offered to let me go with full pay and replace me with a temp, I'd have to be a complete fool to refuse it."

"Exactly." Thank goodness she was regaining control of her good sense.

"But we're not talking about a desk job here," she went on, raising an eyebrow and looking at Charles expectantly.

"No, but it's not as if we're talking about some great specialized position for which you need added experience in order to get the skills to gain a better job the next time around."

She frowned thoughtfully, wrinkling her forehead in a surprisingly cute way. "I don't need more experience in order to get another job as a nanny?"

He shrugged, hoping to reassure her and put that light back in her eyes. "I can't see why."

It came back all right.

"There!" She pointed at him. "Right there, you just admitted I don't need more experience in order to be a nanny. Therefore you can't terminate our contract on the basis of my supposed inexperience." She folded her arms in front of her and gave a nod that clearly said, *Answer that one, Captain Smartypants.*

And she was right, in a way. He'd painted himself into a corner. "I believe what I said was that I preferred someone more *mature.*"

"Older."

"Yes."

"Which adds up to prejudice on the basis of age."

She was good, he had to admit it.

What a gift she had for turning things around to suit her point.

Fortunately, he was no slouch himself. "I'd hate to bring it up under oath," he began. "But the truth is, I wanted someone mature enough—regardless of age—to follow my explicit instructions. For example, if I told them not to take my daughter, unprotected, to a large festival in another town, I'd expect them to not take my daughter, unprotected, to a large festival in another town."

Laurel's cheeks pinkened.

It was actually quite pretty on her.

She sank into the seat opposite him. "You're pretty good at playing your hand."

He smiled—he couldn't help it—and gave a nod of acknowledgment. "So are you."

She sighed. "Look, let's be honest. No veiled threats, no tap-dancing, let me just tell you the truth."

He splayed his arms. "I'm listening."

"Okay. I need a job. There's no denying that. And this job particularly suits my needs because it allows me to live where I want to live, and visit my father during my time off. Those were plusses when I applied for the position."

"Okay…?" Most people would have made their demands already, so Charles was at a disadvantage in dealing with her. Laurel was different. He kept discovering that over and over again.

"But there's also the human element."

"Human element?"

"Penny."

"Oh. Of course." He was a jerk to have not seen it before. Here he was, thinking of everything in such practical, literal, businesslike terms, and in the process he was inadvertently making her point for her. "I thought you meant…" His voice trailed off.

There was no good explanation for what he'd thought she meant.

They both knew what he'd thought she meant.

Fortunately, Laurel didn't just sit there, enjoying his discomfort. She lurched on toward her point. "Whether you agree or not, and you've made it pretty clear you don't, Penny needs emotional support and she needs it *now.* She's lost her mother, and to a lesser extent you—"

"I'm here."

"Sometimes. And sometimes you're not." Laurel's eyes were sharp. Open to his answer, but knowing what it *should* be, all the same. "And when you are here, are you really *interacting* with her?"

No, he wasn't.

They both knew that.

"You've made my point for me," he said. "No, I'm not always here. Often, I have to go to New York, or France, or Italy, or any number of places on business. Wherever wine is a prominent market. So what Penny needs is someone who can be here for the long haul. Someone who has already raised a family, or who has decided she's not *going* to raise her own family. In short, someone who is prepared to make a long-term commitment."

"What makes you think I'm not?" Laurel asked, exasperated.

"You're young, you're beautiful, you're just back in the United States after spending a good chunk of your young years in a third world country in need of reparations." He counted these things off on his fingers. "You haven't even turned thirty yet. You don't *know* what's going to happen in the future." No sooner had he gotten that sentence out than he remembered what the supposed fortune teller had said at the River Witch Festival. It gave him pause for a moment, not because he believed her, but because anyone who'd heard and remembered what she'd said would have to stumble over the phrase *you don't know what's going to happen in the future.*

All he knew was what *wasn't* going to happen in the future. The fortune teller had been dead wrong—he *wasn't* going to spend his life with Laurel Midland.

CHAPTER TEN

"WELL, OF COURSE we don't know what's going to happen in the future," Laurel said to Charles. The Chapawpa psychic's words still rang ominously in her mind's ear, though, reminding her of the psychic in Lenovia.

Was it true that *no one* knew what would happen in the future?

And if some people *did* know, or even *might* know, was it foolish to ignore their warnings?

She couldn't stand to think about it.

"But you don't *need* to see the far distant future in order to know what Penny needs now," she went on. "She needs *me*." Laurel was firm on this point. "And I can assure you I'm not going to fall head over heels for some joker unexpectedly and run off with him."

"You don't know that for certain."

"I can promise you," she said firmly, looking into Charles's eyes, "that I will *not* abandon Penny."

"What if you do fall in love?" he asked.

Her first reaction was that such an idea was crazy, but when she looked at Charles to say it, something in her made her pause. When she looked into his eyes and started to say she'd never fall in love, she couldn't get the words out.

So she overcompensated by giving a derisive snort. "Not likely."

He lifted an eyebrow and—was it her imagination?—looked at her with interest. "No?"

"No."

"Never?"

She swallowed. "Not in the near future."

"How do you know someone isn't going to come along and sweep you off your feet next week?"

She cleared her throat and tried to compose herself. "Mr. Gray, I'm not that easily swept."

"Charles," he corrected.

"Okay, Charles. I don't understand the point of this conversation. One would think you were talking to some flighty girl who had leapt from one crush to another and another. What have I done to give you the impression that I'm so fickle or easily swayed?"

"It's not personal."

"How could it *not* be?"

"At your age, anything could happen," he said, then nodded to himself, as if convincing himself of something even he didn't necessarily believe.

"My age?" she repeated incredulously. You'd think he was talking to a thirteen-year-old! "I'm twenty-eight. I don't think that's very much younger than you."

"You might as well be a hundred years younger than I am," he said wearily, and again she had the impression he was speaking to something inside himself.

"Oh, come on," she said, abandoning any pretense of an employee-employer conversation filter. "What are you, thirty-six?"

"Thirty-eight."

She gave a laugh. "And that makes you too old for things like," she shrugged, "spontaneously falling for someone and running off into the sunset with them?" A little voice in the back of her mind told her she was entering dangerous territory, but it was too late to go back.

He looked her evenly in the eye. "My age doesn't prevent me from doing that."

A tremor of caution crossed her chest. "No?"

"No, my *realism* prevents me from doing that."

"Some might call that cynicism," she said lightly, wondering what his answer would be.

"Would you?"

Until recently, no. Now?

"I'm not sure," she said honestly. "Maybe it's cynical *and* realistic." She shrugged. "I can relate."

He laughed. "I don't believe a woman like you could possibly relate to that."

"Why not?" She wasn't sure whether she should feel insulted by that or not.

"Because you're so passionate about everything."

Her face grew warm. "You think so?"

"Anyone who can work up an argument over the benefits of a Halloween festival as quickly and as strongly as you did is definitely passionate." Something about the way he looked at her gave her the feeling he didn't mean it as a put-down.

"That wasn't about the festival," she said, still feeling the pink in her cheeks and hoping Charles didn't notice. "It was about Penny."

"I know," he said. "I remember what you said." His gaze ran over her, and he took a short breath and started to say something, then stopped and gave a small shake of his head. "This might not be a good time for us to have this conversation."

She was puzzled. "Why not?"

"It's…late." He glanced out the window. It was dark, but only about nine p.m.

Still, Laurel had at least *some* good sense and if he was dismissing her from the room without actually dismissing her from the house after the day they'd had, she should probably let him.

"That's fine," she said, resisting an impulse to add that she thought it was silly and that they should just hash this whole "too young" thing out right now. "I'll see you tomorrow."

He gave a nod. "Tomorrow."

Laurel left, irked by almost everything about Charles Gray: his distant detachment; his stubbornness; his occasional slip off-guard; the rare but devastating smiles he gave her; the way his eyes turned down slightly in the outside corners, making him look like a tortured hero in a romantic movie…

All of it drove her crazy.

She strode through the halls, thinking of all the things that she should have said, if only she'd been able to think just a little faster on her feet.

She should have asked him if he really cared about his daughter's welfare, or if he only cared to *look* like he cared about his daughter's welfare. Because if he *really* cared about what was best for

Penny, he'd set his prejudices aside long enough to see how she was responding to her current situation.

Laurel hadn't been here long but already she adored Penny, and she knew that Penny was very fond of her too. Admittedly, she still had some reservations—a trait she clearly had inherited from her father—but she was warming up to Laurel more and more each day.

It was all about trust, Laurel thought. Penny was learning to trust her. During Laurel's earliest days in the house, Penny had swung manically from loving to mistrusting, accusing Laurel of intending to "leave like everyone else did."

Now if Charles had his way, she was going to do just that. And Penny would never understand that it wasn't about her. This was the kind of thing that would carve itself into her subconscious, making her a mistrustful adult, without ever fully realizing why.

One didn't need to be a psychologist to see that happening or to understand why it would.

It was just so maddening.

Why wouldn't he listen to her?

Because he thought she was young, and that therefore her opinion didn't mean anything? Did he think she was stupid and not worth listening to?

Did he think she was wrong?

Laurel got to Penny's bedroom door and stopped. She hadn't even thought about going to check on the child, it had just come naturally to her. She had to make sure she was okay.

Maybe she needed Penny as much as Penny needed her.

Maybe she needed Penny even *more* than Penny needed her.

She pushed the door open and crept across the low carpet by the light of Penny's stained glass night-light. It was a beautiful thing, but like so many other things in the house, it was too sophisticated for her. Laurel had wanted to replace it with a teddy bear one or something, but Mrs. Daniels had warned her against making any changes to Penny's environment without consulting Charles first.

Laurel had a pretty good idea that consulting Charles about *changing Penny's environment* wouldn't go well.

Now she went over to the bed and looked down at the child who was sleeping so sweetly, the breath whispering in and out of her at an even tempo. Marigold was next to her, and Penny had her thin arm wrapped around the doll.

Her world was so small, yet even so it had already had so many sad and frightening elements.

Laurel just wanted to erase all of that for her.

And maybe some part of Laurel wanted to erase her own painful childhood memories by helping Penny with hers.

She sat down on the edge of the bed and smoothed Penny's hair back off her face.

She wished she could draw, so she could capture this moment and its timeless innocence, and keep it forever.

"Have happy dreams," Laurel whispered, and bent down to kiss Penny's cheek.

The child stirred and rolled over but didn't wake up.

Laurel smiled, and left the room, closing the door behind her and standing in the hallway.

She wasn't going to abandon Penny.

No matter what Charles Gray had in mind, no matter what crazy thoughts he had about hiring some dour old woman with warts on her nose to be Penny's nanny, Laurel was going to *make* him see that no one would be better for the job than she was.

It wasn't even about the money so much anymore, or even the sanctuary of Gray Manor.

It was about Penny.

And if he cared about the child half as much as he purported to, then he was going to *have* to keep Laurel.

CHAPTER ELEVEN

CHARLES GRAY WAS *not* a stubborn man.

Despite his appearances to the contrary lately, he *was* capable of seeing the forest for the trees, even when it came to his daughter and Laurel Midland.

The problem was, Laurel Midland had a way of creating so much chaos in him that he had trouble *admitting* that he saw the forest for the trees.

But he did.

He saw that Penny was growing very close to Laurel. He knew that Penny had a hard time trusting *anyone* enough to get close.

He also knew where she'd gotten that trait.

Laurel had pegged it, all of it. She'd pointed out the fact that Penny was warming to her, and she didn't even have the benefit of knowing Penny had barely given her last three nannies the time of day.

She was never a rude child, of course, but when

she was shy around someone, she was painfully shy. She'd get tongue-tied to the point where she could, or would, barely answer simple questions.

He'd seen her display none of that with Laurel. To the contrary, Penny seemed to be confiding in Laurel about everything from friends to school, and who knows what else? Penny was opening up like a night blooming jasmine, late but not too late.

If he took Laurel from her now, it would be a terrible blow to her heart, and her heart had already had enough of those.

So as impossible as Laurel was, as obstinate and know-it-all-ish and impertinent as she was, he was going to have to let her stay.

In fact, if need be, he was going to have to beg her to stay.

He got up out of his easy chair and walked over to the wet bar in the false backed library shelf, right behind Mark Twain. He flipped it around and started to take the top off the single malt Scotch, but then he stopped. It was strong stuff. With a woman like Laurel in the house, he wanted to keep his wits intact.

He reached instead for a bottle of 2001 cabernet, drew the cork out and poured the ruby liquid into a glass.

What had happened to his life over the past

several weeks? How had everything changed so much so fast?

It would be ironic if the man who had never had to beg a woman for anything in his life had to suddenly do so on behalf of his six-year-old daughter, but if that's what he had to do, he'd do it.

For *her,* he'd do it.

He downed the wine and poured another glass. That turned out to be lucky, too, because no sooner had he closed the shelf bar then Laurel Midland herself came stampeding back into the study.

"Look," she said, without preamble, "I know you value your privacy and that there's probably nothing more inappropriate I could do right now than come back in here after being dismissed and tell you that you're wrong, but I don't see as I have any other choice. You're wrong, Mr.—Charles. Dead wrong."

He looked at her. She looked shaky, though whether it was from the exertion or nervousness, he couldn't say. "About what?" he asked, reasonably certain he already knew the answer.

"About Penny. And, more specifically, about my role in taking care of her."

He raised an eyebrow and waited for her to continue.

She did. Of course. "Now I'm not saying I'm the only person in the world who could have done this job, but, for whatever reason, Penny has taken to me. She trusts me. And I'm not going to let her down." She crossed her arms in front of her. "I'm *not* leaving."

This was interesting.

Charles held back a smile. That, in and of itself, was a reaction he hadn't felt to a woman in a long time. He was enjoying Laurel, he really was. It wasn't everyone who spoke their mind to him.

In fact, it was almost no one who truly spoke their mind to him, at least among his employees.

This was refreshing. Obnoxious, to be sure, but refreshing.

So he decided to string it along.

"Do you like wine?" he asked her.

She was taken aback. "Do I like…wine?"

He got up and went to the Twain shelf. "Mm-hm."

"Are you asking if I have an alcohol problem or if I approve of your family business?"

Charles laughed. "I'm just asking if you like wine." He opened the shelf and took a bottle out.

"I…have some now and then. Not to extremes, but…"

He could almost *see* the thought process.

Approving of the family business beat disapproving of alcohol consumption.

"...sure, I like wine."

"We have a cabernet I'd like your opinion of." He didn't need her opinion. He knew it was excellent. But he really wanted to see her loosen up a little. "Would you like to try some?"

Come to think of it, maybe he'd loosened up a little too much.

Maybe this was a bad idea.

But he couldn't stop. It had just been so damn long since he'd had any kind of personal relationship.

Even an antagonistic one.

"Er..." Laurel looked uncertain.

So he poured. "Go ahead. It's a good year."

"Now or then?" she asked, taking the glass from him.

That remains to be seen, he thought. But he said, "Take your pick. It's good wine, anyway."

She took a sip, closed her eyes for a moment, then said, "Yes. It really is."

God, she was beautiful.

And he hadn't even had that much wine to drink, so this irrational urge he suddenly felt to kiss her could only be blamed on...what? Nature, he supposed.

"What's wrong?" she asked suddenly, taking a step back.

"Nothing." He frowned, trying to collect his thoughts and gather them here in the present. "Nothing at all. Why?"

"The way you were looking at me," she said. "It was…" Her voice trailed off and instead her cheeks went pink. "Nothing."

This was dangerous territory. He was on the verge of kissing this woman, when not long ago he'd been ready to fire her and never see her again.

It was crazy.

He took a step back himself. "I don't mean to make you uncomfortable."

"Oh, it's not that," she said quickly. "It's just…we were talking about Penny, and I know she means the world to you, but I promise you she's already come to mean a lot to me and, while we don't see eye to eye on this—"

"You can stay." Why put her through this? She'd argued until she was blue in the face to keep her position as Penny's nanny, yet here she was, ready to argue the point some more.

It was enough. He'd realized she was right. He couldn't keep stringing her along, no matter how much he enjoyed seeing her pretty face frowning with concern for her job.

Now that concern turned to bewilderment. "What?"

"You heard me."

Bewilderment turned to suspicion. "What do you mean? Yesterday you wanted me gone. There's no way you've changed your mind that fast."

He smiled. "Perhaps you don't read people as well as you like to think you do."

"Maybe I don't." She still looked him over like he was an ancient manuscript she'd found, written in hieroglyphics. "So why don't you tell me exactly what you mean? You want me to stay on as Penny's nanny?"

"Yes."

She looked stunned. Really and truly stunned. But she recovered her composure quickly and someone else might not have picked up on the initial surprise that had registered in her eyes. "For real?" she asked. "Or just for another two weeks, until our contract term is up?"

"For real." Since when did he talk like this? Laurel brought out something in him that he'd rarely—if ever—demonstrated. A sort of…playfulness.

And, honestly, it didn't feel all that bad.

Especially when she looked at him like she did

right now, with her eyes wide open, and that pretty mouth twitching into a wide, white smile. "Really?"

He gave a nod. "Yes." But, being Charles Gray, he couldn't help but add, "As long as you follow my wishes, as regards my daughter." Even to his own ears, his words sounded stilted and overly formal.

"Oh, of course!" Laurel enthused, wholly without irony. She must have been so glad to get the news she's been lobbying for that she didn't care how it was presented.

"That won't be a problem?" Charles hammered. "Doing what I instruct, I mean, even if it goes against your increasingly-infamous instincts?"

"Absolutely." She made the sign of crossing her heart. "Whatever you say goes."

"Good."

But surely they both knew that was going to be quite a challenge for her.

Charles poured more wine. He needed it. "I agree with you that Penny needs some constants in her life, and she's not getting them from me. I travel quite a lot, and besides that I'm..." What? How could he explain the strange shyness he had with his own daughter?

It would sound like madness to an outsider.

"You're...planning to work on your relationship

with Penny?" Laurel finished for him, a smile pulling at her pretty lips.

He wanted to see that smile. "Yes." He had to smile himself. "If that's what you need to hear, then, yes." He couldn't help it, he wanted to goad her into goading him. He wanted her to tease him, to flirt, to bat those beautiful green eyes and smile that warm and sexy smile.

He stepped forward, looking into her eyes.

Like something from a movie, she did the same, holding his gaze and returning it boldly.

Without thinking—without a doubt, thinking would have stopped him—he moved forward, pulled her into his arms, and captured her mouth with his.

And she kissed him right back.

The sensation of her mouth beneath his, and her body forming to his, wrapping herself around him, was instantly overwhelming. Her softness molded against the hard contours of his body, touching a small flame to an unlit match that had lingered within him for too long.

It was like nothing he'd ever felt before—this release, this longing, this need, and this satisfaction, all at once, adding up like some grand mathematical problem into the sum of his needs.

He needed Laurel.

How had *that* happened? She was supposed to be there for his daughter, a generic helper who had nothing to do with the way he spent his days.

When—and how—had she become the one thing he wanted to plan his day around?

He drew back from her, breathing like a boxer who had just gone three rough rounds, and looked into her gemlike eyes, trying to find the answer to a question he couldn't articulate.

A moment stretched between them as they looked at each other, communicating and yet not communicating.

Then, without warning, she leaned into him again, and his mouth was on hers again, probing, exploring, wanting more, and more, and more.

There was no thought, just instinct. He ran his hands up her back, spanning it with his hands. She was so delicate and yet so strong. When they'd argued, she'd seemed like she was tall and strong but now, in his arms, she seemed as slight as a rag doll.

Charles lowered one hand to her lower back and pulled her closer, feeling the warmth of her against him even through their clothes.

And he kissed her again.

And she kissed him again.

And time seemed to stand still as they melted together.

Finally, she pushed back away from him, her face flushed. "This…we can't do this."

"I know."

A moment shivered between them.

She took one more step back and swallowed. "We have a professional relationship. This could really…" She was still breathless. "Complicate things."

"I agree." And he did, on principle. And in the morning, after he'd gotten some much-needed sleep, he was sure he'd agree even more. "I apologize if I acted inappropriately."

If?

"No, no, I'm not saying—" She looked down, then met his eyes again. Her pupils were so large they made her normally-pale eyes look black. "It's just that—" She shrugged. "It must be the wine."

"That's it, the wine."

She gave a coquettish smile. "Gray Manor Vineyards. There's something about it."

"We should use that as an advertisement."

She smiled. "You'd probably make a lot of sales with it."

Their eyes held for a moment.

"I sincerely do apologize," Charles said. "I assure

you that's never happened before." Wait, that sounded wrong. "I mean, with any of the nannies. Or any of the hired help." He was making a mess of this. What was it about Laurel Midland that made him feel and act like such a damn fool?

"It's okay." She smiled. "I understand what you're saying."

He gave a brief but grateful smile. "Then we'll let it go. I promise you it won't happen again."

Was it his imagination or did something like disappointment fall into her expression?

Whatever it was, it was gone in an instant and Laurel nodded. "I'm going back upstairs now. Thanks so much for understanding and keeping me on here. You won't be sorry."

God, he hoped not.

But something told him there was more trouble coming.

CHAPTER TWELVE

THERE WAS NEVER A TIME when Laurel missed her best friend more.

Certainly there had been many dark nights when she'd thought about her, and thought about the horror of what had happened. The pain of those thoughts was extreme, but it was different from the pain of missing her, and usually she tried not to allow herself the indulgence of missing her when the loss was so much bigger and more tragic than that.

Her name had been Laurel too. Their group had teased them about being "the Laurels" or "the flowers". Both had worked teaching English to children, so with their jobs being interchangeable, a lot of people felt like they themselves were also interchangeable.

That had turned out to be more true than Laurel ever could have anticipated.

But now she didn't want to think about the sadness and the loss. She just wanted to sit down with her friend over bad black coffee like they used to and talk about the romantic feelings she suddenly found herself having for Charles Gray.

When she'd first met him, he'd struck her as impossibly cold and detached. And, of course, broodingly handsome. There was no denying that element of Heathcliffe he possessed.

No sooner had he barked at her that she was fired, then she found herself wondering what motivated him, where the pain was that made him so chilly, and what it would take to heal it.

Of course it hadn't been her first impulse to heal it *herself*. She had only wondered about it.

But as she'd gotten to know him better over the weeks, she'd come to understand that he was lonely. And he was smart, and funny, and strong, and, heaven knew, he was handsome.

So Laurel had found herself thinking about him more and more. Noticing him in Penny's facial expressions or gestures. That was the kicker. There was so much of him in Penny but they didn't spend enough time together. If there was one thing Laurel needed to accomplish in her time with Penny, it was that she needed to help Penny and Charles forge more of a relationship.

Which was why, when Penny's school sent a note home that there would be a fall fundraising event involving a silent auction and concert by the children, Laurel immediately set her mind to getting Charles to go.

"It's tonight?" he said when she told him about it.

They were in his office and she'd waited until early afternoon so that he'd have enough time to finish whatever he was working on for the day, but not so much time that he could come up with an excuse to get out of going.

"I could have used more notice," he said.

"If I'd given you more notice you would have used it to get out of going," Laurel said confidently.

"Get out of going?" A shade of guilt came over his face. "Why would you say that?"

"Well, I can't help but notice you don't seem to like crowds."

"Who does?"

"No, I mean you *really* don't like crowds."

He put his pen down on his desk, and leaned back, looking at Laurel, who stood before him. "Do you?"

"I don't *hate* them. I don't actually avoid leaving the house in order to avoid them."

"Neither do I."

"Then why don't you ever go to any of Penny's school events? Dare I even mention the River Witch Festival?"

"I wouldn't if I were you."

Okay, so that would be a bad idea. Still, her point remained. She believed he loved his child, he didn't avoid these events out of an aggressive desire to not be around her. "So why don't you ever go to her school events?"

"Who says I don't?" he countered.

"I, personally, have already been to two of them this month," Laurel said. "The piano recital and *Magic in the Toy Shop.*" At the question in his eyes, she explained, "The fall play. You didn't get to see Penny be a Twister box in her theater debut."

Charles smiled, and it touched his eyes with melancholy. "I would have liked to have seen that."

"Then come tonight and see her sing solo in *The Scarecrow Under the Harvest Moon,*" Laurel urged.

"What does that mean?"

"It's one of the songs for the fall concert. They're not allowed to do anything relating to Halloween—too pagan—or Thanksgiving, which apparently not everyone celebrates. So instead they have a concert full of bad songs no one ever heard of, devoted to things like the moon and squash, and falling leaves." She laughed. "Come on, it will be fun."

He met her eyes. "I'll have to check my schedule."

"Check you—" She pulled up a chair and sat down in front of him. "What's really going on?"

He looked at her, then at the chair, then back at her. But he didn't comment on her making herself at home. Instead he just said, "I don't know what you mean."

"Why don't you want to go?"

He sighed and leaned back, steepling his hands in front of him. She was onto him, and he knew her well enough to know that she wasn't going to let up until she had her answers. So he gave it to her.

The truth.

"I never know what I'm supposed to do at those things."

She frowned. "What do you mean?"

"Angelina was very involved in the school stuff. Even when Penny was in preschool, Angelina knew all the other players and went to all the fundraisers and events. She's the one who picked the school, and she wanted Penny to have the advantage, whatever advantage there was, of having gone to Pendleton Primary School." He shrugged. "Angelina was all about that stuff. I never got involved."

"Well, I think it's time you did." She smiled, and resisted the urge to reach out and take his hands in hers. "Look, I've never had a child of my own, so this is all new to me too, but it's not that big a deal. You just go where they tell you, do what everyone else is doing, and enjoy watching your daughter perform."

He looked dubious. "Does it matter that much to Penny?"

Laurel recalled Penny's earnest little face when she'd asked, *Do you think my father will come? Can you ask him?* and said, without a doubt, "Yes, it *really* matters to her."

He gave a nod. "Then I'll go."

"Good." Laurel stood up to go.

"Are you planning to go?"

She was. "If I say yes, are you planning to use that as an excuse *not* to go at the last minute?"

He laughed. "You're a sharp one, I've got to hand it to you."

She smiled and tried to ignore the fluttering in her chest as she turned and walked away, feeling his eyes on her.

The concert was adorable. The sound of those little voices raised in song—even songs about Grandfather Oak and The One-Eyed Sparrow who

Saved a Pumpkin Patch—was so touching that several times Laurel had had to fight back tears.

"When's Penny's solo?" Charles whispered in Laurel's ear, sending shivers across her entire body.

"I'm not sure," she whispered back. "Why?"

"My phone keeps ringing. I need to take the call."

She gave him an exasperated look, but he was facing the stage, so she had to add, "It's not like this is *La Boheme.*"

"You're telling me."

"I'm sure it will be over soon."

It was, but not before Penny had gotten up and forgotten the words in her solo. The poor thing had looked so horrified that her cheeks glowed like neon, even back where Laurel sat in the audience.

When Laurel glanced at Charles, she could see his eyes were fastened on his daughter, his jaw tight with sympathy.

"Maybe we should stop for ice cream on the way home," Laurel whispered.

He glanced at her and gave a short smile. "Definitely."

They watched the remainder of the concert in companionable silence, sitting side-by-side in the darkened auditorium, their arms and legs just inches apart.

Every now and then, when one of them would move, they'd bump arms or knees, and each time, Laurel felt it like it was an electrical shock shooting through her.

She didn't know what it was about this man, but she was having feelings that were increasingly difficult to ignore.

This became even more evident later that evening on the way home, when Penny began crying in the back seat.

"What's wrong, honey?" Laurel asked, unsnapping her seat belt and turning to face the child.

"I forgot my song."

"Did you?" Laurel asked guilelessly. She'd been waiting for this to come up, and was surprised it had taken this long.

Penny was surprisingly adept at holding emotions inside, especially for a child her age.

Penny sniffled and nodded. "I forgot."

"I didn't notice that," Laurel said, then looked at Charles. "Did you?"

He shook his head. "I thought you sang beautifully."

"You—you *did?*" Penny asked, blinking hard.

"Are you kidding?" Charles said. "You were the best one there. I could hear you over everyone."

"Really?" Penny looked so pleased that the tears that still lingered on her cheeks looked like a mistake.

"Did you know your great-great-grandmother Lucinda was a singer?" he asked her.

"Who is she?"

"She was my father's grandmother," Charles explained. "And she was famous all over the world for her singing voice. People would come from miles and miles away just to hear her perform."

Laurel was surprised to hear this. "Not Lucinda Moricelli."

Charles gave her a surprised glance. "That's right. You've heard of her?"

"Absolutely."

"I didn't think anyone knew who she was anymore."

Laurel was astonished. "My father used to listen to her records all the time. I mean *all* the time. Those old 78's."

"Your *father* had those?" Charles asked. 78's had predated CD's and LP's by decades, most people probably wouldn't have known what they were if they'd seen them. "He must have been a hundred and twelve when you were born."

"They were out of date even for my dad," Laurel explained. "I think they belonged to *his* grandparents.

But he had one of those old record players and that was all that would play on it." She shook her head, remembering. Lucinda Moricelli's haunting voice had been the soundtrack of Laurel's childhood. "Do you have them? And something to play them on?"

"Somewhere, probably."

"Oh, Penny." She looked back at the child. "Wait until you hear your great-great grandmother sing!"

"I want to! I want to! Can we do it when we get home?"

Laurel looked to Charles. "Think you can put your hands on them easily?"

He drew the car to a stop at a red light and she saw him frown in the red glow. "I think they're in the attic. I couldn't swear to it, but I'm pretty sure, so," he glanced in the rear view mirror, and smiled. "Yes, I think so. Probably."

Penny clapped excitedly, her own humiliation on stage a long distant memory. "Can we go right home and get ice cream tomorrow? I want to hear my great-grandmother."

Laurel smiled at the fact that Penny was careful to keep ice cream in the future instead of abandoning the idea altogether. "Let's do it."

An hour later, Penny was in her pajamas and had dutifully cleaned her face, hands, and teeth, but Charles still hadn't emerged from the attic with the records.

Penny yawned. "I'm tired. Is he almost back?"

"I'm sure he is," Laurel said. Charles had gone to the attic entrance in the back of the house half an hour earlier and they hadn't heard from him since. "But why don't you just lie down and relax," she suggested, leading the girl to her bed. "If you fall asleep we can listen to the records in the morning."

"Don't I have school?"

Laurel shook her head. "It's Saturday."

"Oh." Penny yawned again, then rolled over and pulled the covers up close to her chin. Within seconds, it seemed, she'd closed her eyes and was breathing the steady, even breath of sleep.

Laurel smiled to herself, and kissed Penny's cheek. It had been a long night. Penny had gone through a wide spectrum of emotions, from nervousness about going on the stage, to embarrassment at forgetting the words, to the excitement of finding out her great-grandmother had been a singer that she could actually listen to.

No wonder she was exhausted.

CHAPTER THIRTEEN

THE ATTIC WAS LIKE SOMETHING from a children's book of magic, full of dust and spider webs and the smell of must.

When he was a kid, Charles had enjoyed coming up here and searching through the old stuff. There were generations' worth, some things dating back as far as the Civil War. He'd often told himself that someday, when he had time, he was going to sort through it all. There were probably some real treasures here.

Unfortunately, at the moment, he couldn't find the one thing he was looking for: the wooden crate that housed the collected operas performed by Lucinda Moricelli.

"Charles?"

Laurel's voice surprised him. He'd never been up here with anyone else, but he'd always half-expected to be visited by a ghost, so when he heard Laurel, it gave him a start.

"I'm sorry, I didn't meant to scare you," she said, creeping through the attic. "I just wanted to tell you there's no hurry. Penny fell asleep. She was exhausted."

He nodded. "I thought she was going to conk out in the car."

"It didn't take long." Laurel looked around at the shadows cast by one lone light bulb, probably from 1942, hanging tenuously from a wire in the roof. "It's spooky up here."

Charles nodded thoughtfully. "I could hire someone to organize it, put up fluorescent lights and cabinets, and so on, but I think I prefer it this way."

"I don't blame you." There was a real atmosphere to this place. It had the most *lived-in* feel in the whole house. Well, that and a certain element of *died-in* feel, though she doubted—she hoped—that was the case. "But it is like something from a ghost story up here. I wouldn't want to come in here alone."

"I used to do it all the time."

"Yeah?" She pictured him coming up here from his office and…what? She couldn't see it.

"When I was a kid," he explained. "This was a hell of an escape for a kid."

"Oh, I can imagine." And she could. She could totally picture that. She ran her hand across the old Victrola, then blew the dust off her fingertips. "Haven't used this in awhile, huh?"

He looked at her and chuckled. "Most of the music I like comes on CD these days."

She laughed, and opened the lid of the old machine. "It's actually pretty clean inside," she noted, bending down to examine it more closely. "Do you have a record we can put on?"

"That's what I'm looking for now." He pushed aside an ancient scrap book, and the edges of some of the pages crackled off and fluttered to the floor.

"Where should I help look?"

"Maybe in that box," he said, gesturing toward a trunk under a high round window. "I know they're here because I've seen them, and no one comes up here who could have thrown them out."

"I can't believe you don't have them out so you can listen to them," Laurel said, picking her way across the dusty wood planks to the trunk that looked like it might contain an actual skeleton.

Charles stopped digging for a moment and looked at her. "I don't crank up the old Victrola that often."

She laughed. "Well, maybe you should. What a cool thing that is." She gingerly opened the trunk, honestly afraid something might jump out at her, but it was only a collection of books and—there they were—neatly stacked piles of Lucinda Moricelli's recordings. "Oh, look! I found them!"

"You did?" Charles put down the box he was about to open and came over to her.

Laurel carefully lifted out a few of the records. "Wow, they look like they're in perfect condition."

He bent over her and picked some up. The clean smell of soap touched her nostrils and made her want to reach out to him. "They really haven't seen much use," he said, drawing back with a couple in his hands. "I don't even know what all of them are." He held them out to her. "Got an opinion?"

She chose one that she recognized from her father's collection. "Try this."

He took it over to the Victrola, cranked the handle, put the heavy needle down on the album and—*voila!*—music.

The voice was so clear, so emotional, so deep that almost immediately Laurel started to cry.

"Hey, what's wrong?" Charles asked, coming over to her. "What's the matter?"

"Nothing?" She smiled and sniffed. "I'm fine it's just…it's so beautiful."

"Do you always cry when you're happy?"

She nodded. "Sometimes."

He smiled and touched his fingertips to her cheek. "I think that's sweet."

She looked into his eyes. She wanted him to kiss her so much that she almost couldn't stand it.

It went against everything she knew was right in employer-employee relationships. They needed to be professional, to have distance between them, to work together for the good of Penny and not for their own mutual desires, but…darn, she really hoped he'd kiss her.

And he didn't let her down.

He lowered his mouth onto hers, just as he had before, only this time it was somehow even more intoxicating. Because this time, he'd done it before, and they'd backed off before, but he was doing it again.

Which had to mean—didn't it?—that he was finding it as difficult to resist her as she was finding it to resist him.

As if in affirmation, he lowered his mouth onto hers and gathered her into his arms, pulling her close against the hard contours of his body.

She couldn't think.

And she didn't want to.

All she could do was let go.

She allowed the blissful sensation of his kiss to

swirl her into its warmth. The experience was dizzying, yet when she concentrated on Charles, she was centered. Everything was right.

At least for the moment.

She wasn't going to let this go too far. She wouldn't enter territory she couldn't retreat from. After all, he was still her boss. She needed to remember that.

And she tried, she truly tried, as she trailed her hands slowly across the muscles of his back and across his shoulder blades.

Charles drew her closer in response, pressing his palms against her lower back, making her hyper-aware of every part of him. She felt his belt buckle pressing against her stomach and tried to stop herself from imagining what was beneath.

No sooner could she entertain the thought then, instinctively, he deepened the kiss, running his tongue across her lower lip and probing gently inside her mouth. She responded hungrily, move for move.

Then he kissed her cheek, then her temple, and held her, his face against her hair. "I've never felt quite like this," he murmured.

"Neither have I."

"Should we stop?"

She drew a short breath. Of course they should stop. But *could* she?

No way.

"A little more," she said, kissing his mouth.

He responded with enthusiasm, ending the conversation for now by exploring her with his mouth.

She leaned her head back, and he trailed kisses across her jaw line and down her throat.

"Should we go to my room?" he asked against her skin.

"If we do, we'll be sorry," she said. "I think."

"You're probably right." He kissed her mouth and for a moment she sank against him, temptation taunting her.

She wanted more.

But she couldn't.

Because if she went any further, she'd reach a point of emotional attachment she would *not* be able to back away from. Already she had stronger feelings for Charles Gray than she'd ever had for any man, but even so she'd experienced enough pain and heartbreak to last her a lifetime. She didn't want to invest herself so fully in someone she was still so unsure of.

So she drew back. "We need to talk."

"We do?" he murmured. It was as if he was still intoxicated from their encounter.

She could understand that. That's why she

wanted to change the subject. "Yes." She swallowed. "There's a big week coming up."

"There is?"

She stepped back and pulled up a box to sit on. "Yes, of course. Thanksgiving."

He drew a blank. "Thanksgiving?"

"Yes." She looked at him expectantly. *"Thanksgiving,"* she repeated, as if that would somehow make it clearer. "It's next week, you know." Then, when he didn't immediately respond, she added, "Next Thursday."

He searched his memory. He was going to Napa on Thursday. "I'll be out of town. I'm leaving that day."

"You're kidding."

"No, I'm not."

She looked incredulous. "You're leaving *on Thanksgiving day* and you didn't even realize it? How can you travel on the worst travel day of the year and not even know it?"

He shrugged. "When you fly out of a private airport the holiday crowds don't mean anything." But he did realize it was poor timing. "Look, I usually give the staff the time off and Penny and I go to *Chez Rousse* for dinner." Then, knowing Laurel would be all about the importance of the holiday, he added, "It's been our tradition."

He should have known that wouldn't cut it for her.

Laurel's jaw dropped. "Your *tradition* is to take your daughter to a *French* restaurant for *Thanksgiving?*"

He nodded. "It's about family, right? Not what you eat or where you eat it."

"Yes, it's about family," she said. "But it's also about turkey and gravy and mashed potatoes, and yams, and green bean casserole and pumpkin pie and—"

"Gorging yourself."

"*Yes!* With your loved ones. At *home.* Where you can undo the top button of your pants after you've eaten without worrying they're going to drop off in front of a bunch of strangers."

He had to laugh. "While I appreciate the insight into the Midland family priorities, I think *Chez Rousse* will do just fine. I'll have my secretary make you reservations." It was clearly on the tip of her tongue to object, but he raised an eyebrow and added, "I appreciate your making things go so smoothly. For Penny's sake."

Again, she started to speak, but then obviously thought better of it and said, "Not a problem." She took a short breath. "I should get back downstairs now. In case Penny wakes up."

He gave a nod. "Fine." He didn't want her to go, but if he asked her to stay he couldn't be responsible for whatever might happen next. "I'll bring the records downstairs and you can play them for her tomorrow if she's interested."

"She's very interested. I think you should come too, and tell her whatever you can remember about your great-grandmother."

"I never met her," he said, and he regretted it. "She died before I was born. And the truth is, my father hardly ever talked about her. The only reason I know anything about her at all is because I found the records up here when I was a kid."

Laurel looked at him, her eyes large and heavy with pity. "That's sad. But even if you can't tell Penny personal anecdotes about her ancestor, you can play the records for her and tell her what you do know. That sense of history would be good for her, I think."

It had certainly done him some good. "I'll give you the records and the players tomorrow. You can play them for her."

She met his eyes and held them. "I will."

He looked right back at her. "Good."

A long few moments passed between them, long enough for Charles to decide and *un*decide to go to

Laurel several times. Eventually he decided to leave things as they were, for fear of going to her and not being able to get back.

"Thanks for everything you did tonight," he said, stepping back and making a show of looking idly through one of the boxes. He glanced at her. "You were a real help. Penny's lucky to have you here." It was on the tip of his tongue to add *I'm lucky to have you here* but he squelched the urge.

"I'm glad to be here," she said, nodding and looking so deeply into his eyes he thought she could see his soul. After another moment, she said, "I'm going downstairs now. Good night, Charles."

He wanted to tell her to stay, but he had nothing to back it up. Just a lot of hollow desire and neediness. What good would *that* do? "Good night, Laurel," he said, relishing the sound of it. "I'll see you tomorrow."

CHAPTER FOURTEEN

"I CAN'T TELL YOU HOW GREAT it is to see you again!" Lily hugged her sister for the hundredth time since they'd gotten to Rose's duplex overlooking Central Park. Lily didn't even care about the magnificent view, she was totally focused on Rose. "How are you feeling? Here, sit down, take it easy."

"I'm fine." Rose laughed. "I'm pregnant, not made of glass."

In just the two months since Lily had seen her, Rose had…well, she'd bloomed. She absolutely beamed with happiness. Clearly marriage to Warren Harker suited her.

Initially, Lily had worried about her sister's choice of a husband, but he'd won Lily over just as surely as he'd won Rose over. It had turned out the two girls from Brooklyn weren't so different from the billionaire developer. Warren had spent time in the very same orphanage they had been in themselves, and though he'd been adopted out before they ever got to know him, he'd never forgotten the place.

That was probably why, once he'd found out there had been a third sister but she'd been adopted, he'd been absolutely determined to find out where she was.

The sisters gabbed for half an hour about Rose's pregnancy, how she'd taken the test, and how she'd intended to wait until Warren got back from his business trip in order to tell him, but she hadn't been able to wait even ten minutes before calling him.

Then the conversation turned back to the real reason they were here.

"So tell me all about this Laurel Midland," Lily said. "Have you talked to her?"

"No," Rose said, and her expression clouded. "It sounds like she might have some…issues."

Lily didn't like the sound of that. "What issues? What does that mean?"

"I don't know exactly. But apparently she just flipped out when our Laurel died. She disappeared the same night and came back to the States."

"Maybe they were just really good friends and she didn't know how to handle it," Lily suggested. "Grief can do strange things to a person."

Rose nodded. "Or maybe she was afraid for her own life."

It was as if a minor chord chimed in Lily's head. "Why would she be? Laurel was in an accident, wasn't she?"

Rose shook her head and her eyes filled with tears. "Maybe not. The director, his name is Mike by the way, said that Laurel had ticked off some sort of local Russian mafia types. They were using kids as drug runners and she was trying to get their authorities and even our state department to do something about it." Tears spilled down over Rose's cheeks now. "They thought her jeep went over the embankment and exploded, but further investigation has made them think that maybe the jeep exploded first. It was sabotage."

Lily was horrified. Too shocked to share her sister's tears. "Are they doing anything about it?"

"What can they do?"

"Get the guys responsible, that's what. And are they sure Laurel Midland is okay? If she just disappeared and they were such close friends, then maybe—"

"No, he's sure. She left a note, and Warren's investigator has tracked her by her social security number to Gray Manor Vineyards upstate. She's working as a nanny for Charles Gray's child."

Now Lily was beginning to understand. "And you don't want to call her for fear of scaring her off."

"Exactly." Rose nodded. "If we say we want to talk to her about Laurel Standish, she might just think we have something to do with whoever killed Laurel."

"And Laurel would never have told her about us because she didn't know. It would sound like the worst made-up story ever."

"Yup."

"So we ambush her?"

"In a manner of speaking. If we go to talk to her directly she'll undoubtedly see we're on the up and up just by looking at us." Rose gave a humorless laugh. "At least, I hope she will."

"I bet we look like Laurel. Our Laurel, I mean. That might reassure her too."

"Good point."

"So what about the drug runners?"

"Ah." Rose leaned back and looked pleased for the first time in this conversation. "Warren pulled some strings. With Mike's help, the authorities are closing in on the guys."

"And just like that, the problem Laurel died for is solved." It was so sad. Lily and Rose had both spent a long, long time without two dimes to rub together, and she was constantly amazed how efficiently problems could be solved when one was wealthy and powerful. It was unfair, to be sure, but she had to be glad that they could at least do this one thing.

"At least we can do that for Laurel," Rose said, echoing Lily's thoughts.

"At least." She'd handled the flight just fine, but this sad news about her sister's senseless death at the hands of criminals made her feel overwhelmed. She suppressed a yawn, but Rose picked up on it.

"You must be exhausted," Rose said, ending the conversation. "Enough sad talk for tonight, let's get you to bed. We'll come up with a plan for meeting Laurel Midland tomorrow."

CHAPTER FIFTEEN

SURE ENOUGH, CHARLES LEFT Thanksgiving morning without so much as a regretful look back.

At least, that's the way it appeared to Laurel.

Admittedly, she was really beginning to regret any time he wasn't around, though, so she might not be the best judge of what was right and what was wrong.

Not that she needed, or wanted, him there all the time. Much of her day was taken up with the care of Penny and there was no room in the midst of that for romance. Nor would she have wanted to try and make it so. When she was taking care of Penny, she was content to do just that. Honestly, the child brought so much joy to her life that she wasn't entirely sure how she'd ever get along without her.

Indeed, she wasn't sure how she ever *had* gotten along without her.

So when Charles left with instructions that she

take Penny to *Chez Rousse,* Laurel had been looking for any excuse to get out of it. Fortunately, Mother Nature had accommodated her.

The weather report was dreary. Sloppy wet snow, and lots of it. Driving would be treacherous. And there was no way in the world that Laurel would take a chance driving in bad weather with that precious cargo, so as soon as she heard the weather report, she'd called Penny to the car and taken her to the grocery store to get "supplies," "just in case".

Well, "just in case" had begun about 1:30 in the afternoon on Thanksgiving, falling from the sky in great icy wet chunks.

Fortunately, the "supplies" Laurel had picked up had included a sixteen pound turkey, a bag of Idaho potatoes, four yams, a bag of marshmallows, frozen green beans and those fried onions that went on top, along with chicken broth, mushroom soup, heat-n-eat rolls, and a frozen pumpkin pie. She was good, but not so good that she could cook an entire Thanksgiving dinner by herself in a few hours.

As she'd hoped, the snow grew heavier as the afternoon wore on, and there didn't appear to be any hope of it letting up.

What a relief.

Miles came in as Laurel was setting out all of the

ingredients she was going to need. "Blizzard's coming," he said. "Do you want me to get anything from the shop for you before I leave for the weekend?"

"No, Miles, we've got everything we need. Thanks."

"Looks like you're going to cook a big meal."

Laurel looked at the spread and nodded her agreement. "I bought way too much for two people."

"It won't go to waste. Turkey sandwiches, you know." He gave a creaky laugh.

She joined him. "For weeks."

"The missus never cooked, you know," he said, unexpectedly.

What Missus? His? "I'm sorry?"

"Mrs. Gray. Never came near the kitchen." He eyed her keenly. "I think Mr. Gray will be impressed to learn this about you."

Laurel's face went warm. "You do, huh?"

Miles gave a nod. "I've worked here for fifty years now," he said. "I've seen a lot of people come and go, servants, children, wives. And in all that time, Miss, I've never seen anything quite like the way Mr. Gray looks at you. If you'll forgive my saying so."

Laurel's breath caught in her throat. "You must be mistaken. Mr. Gray looks at me as an employee, like any other."

Miles laughed again. "That is not the case, Miss Laurel. That is not the case at all." He gave her a nod, still chuckling, and said, "Happy Thanksgiving to you."

"Happy Thanksgiving." She watched him go, wondering how to think about this revelation he had just given her.

It wasn't as if she thought he was toying with her. He had no way of knowing how much it would mean to her to think she brought some joy to Charles that he hadn't had before.

It just seemed too much to hope for.

So she decided to put it out of her mind, as best she could, and concentrate on making this the best Thanksgiving Penny ever had. Charles she could—and would, if previous nights were any indication—think about later.

At 1:45 p.m. Laurel rubbed butter, salt, pepper, and celery salt on the turkey and put it in the oven.

At 2:30 p.m., as the delicious scent began wafting into the kitchen, she called *Chez Rousse* and cancelled her reservation.

By 3:30 p.m., the kitchen smelled of roasted turkey, giblet gravy, mashed potatoes with cream and bleu cheese, and back-of-the-box recipe for Green Bean Casserole.

"Is this how the pilgrims did it?" Penny asked, pulling a browned marshmallow off the top of the mashed sweet potatoes.

"Sort of," Laurel said, taking another marshmallow for herself. "The spirit's the same."

"The pilgrims didn't have marshmallows, did they?"

"No." Laurel pulled another one off the top of the sweet potatoes. "But I bet they wish they had."

"I've *never* had this for Thanksgiving dinner," Penny said excitedly. "I always have *onion soup au gratin* and *filet mignon.*"

"Steak and soup, huh?" Laurel shook her head. "This is way more in the spirit of things."

And it was. Even though it was just the two of them there, pulling burned marshmallows off the top of a Pyrex pan of sweet potatoes, Laurel had never had such a wonderful Thanksgiving.

"Do you remember what the fortune teller at the River Witch Festival said to my father?" Penny asked.

Laurel tried *not* to think about the River Witch Festival, if she could, so she wasn't sure what Penny was referring to. "What?"

"She said that he was going to marry you."

Laurel felt her face go hot. "I don't think she said that."

"She *did,*" Penny insisted. "Or something like that. She said he was going to spend his life with you."

"She was just an actress," Laurel said, suddenly feeling like ants were crawling under her skin. "She was just playing a game."

Penny looked confused. "She was not! She was right. You and my father are getting married."

"No, honey, we're not." Where was this coming from?

"Yes, you are! I know it!" Penny's voice was rising into the range of hysteria.

"Okay, okay, shhhh." Laurel put a hand on Penny's shoulder. "Calm down. You're taking this too far. The gypsy at the festival was only there to play a game. She wasn't predicting the real future. No one knows what's going to happen in the future."

Penny considered this for a moment, before asking, "So it *might* happen? You *might* marry my father?"

A month ago, Laurel would have been astonished at her own impulse to say *maybe* to this question, but she was smart enough to know that it took two to make a marriage, and one of these two wasn't even considering such a thing.

"No, honey," she said. "I'm here for you, not for your father."

"But he needs you too!" Penny insisted. "He's way happier when you're here."

"Really?" Laurel couldn't help but ask.

Penny nodded enthusiastically. "He never talked to any of my other nannies, but he's always talking to you. And sometimes he asks me where you are. He never did that."

A warm flush filled Laurel. Could there really be something growing between her and Charles?

Was there even a *chance* that his feelings for her were growing in the way hers were for him?

"Your father's a nice man," Laurel understated. "But I don't want you to start hoping something's going to happen between him and me. Like I said, I'm here for you."

Penny looked like she didn't believe that for a second. "The fortune teller said you're going to be my new mommy."

"No, she didn't say *that,* she said—" Laurel stopped. She was *not* going to repeat word for word—although she could—the predictions of a faux psychic at a Halloween party. "Honestly, honey, it was just a game. It wasn't real."

Penny accepted that with a skeptical nod, but she still said, "Daddy will be home soon, we'll ask him then."

Laurel didn't have the heart to point out that, no, her father would *not* be home since he was jet-bound to a vineyard in the Napa Valley. Instead she just said, "We'll see."

So an hour and a half later, when the turkey was done and the marshmallows on top of the sweet potatoes were totally burned, Laurel had the chance to get the answers from the man himself.

Because at 5:15 p.m., despite everything he'd said about the holidays not meaning anything to him, Charles Gray walked into the house.

"You look surprised," Charles said, in the face of the pale, wide-eyed shock Laurel displayed the moment he walked in.

"I wasn't expecting you." Her heart was pounding. For a moment, all of his dire predictions about people wanting to target Penny had come to her mind and she'd wondered wildly if she'd forgotten to lock the door, thereby leaving the way open for just anyone to walk in.

"The wind was too strong to take off." He frowned and looked at the counter, which was full of the evidence of her cooking. "I thought you were going to *Chez Rousse*."

"I was worried that the streets might freeze overnight."

He gave a nod and said, "Good call." He walked over to the counter and picked up a slice of apple she had set out with cheese for Penny. "So you cook too?"

"Yes."

"If we'd hired you to be a cook in the first place we wouldn't have had so many problems." He smiled.

Her heart took off pounding again, but this time it was for a whole different reason. "Are you saying you regret taking me on as Penny's nanny?"

He took another slice of apple. "Believe it or not, I am *not* saying that."

"Wow. Wonders never cease." The wind howled outside, pressing against the window panes along the kitchen wall.

It was so cozy inside, so warm, that Laurel thought she'd never been so at peace.

Penny came running in. "Daddy!" She threw herself into his arms, something Laurel had never seen her do before.

He wrapped his arms around her and lifted her into the air. "Thanksgiving dinner at home. What do you think of that?"

"It's *fun!*" Penny trilled. "Laurel's a really good cook!"

"I'm sure she is." He gave Penny a squeeze, then set her down.

"Can I go back and watch *The Sound of Music* now?" Penny asked. "It's on TV."

"Sure. Go." He ruffled her hair.

When Penny had gone, he turned to Laurel. "Looks like you've performed something of a miracle in the few short weeks that you've been here."

"I don't know about *that,*" she said, wanting to hear more. "But Penny's definitely getting more comfortable."

Charles approached her, advancing until he was just inches away from her.

"You've been amazing."

She swallowed. "You do okay yourself."

"I think it's time for us to talk about something other than your work here," he said, then bent down to kiss her.

His lips grazed lightly across hers at first, then he drew back and looked into her eyes.

Laurel's heart pounded so hard she thought it might burst, and she leaned into him and kissed him back. He wrapped his arms around her, pulling her closer against him.

His tongue touched hers, sending a tremble of pleasure and thrill bubbling through her. The first time he'd kissed her could have been curiosity, the second time might have been a moment of weakness, but this was the third time and there was no other explanation than that he wanted to be with her.

She wrapped her arms around his neck and shoulders, and pulled him closer to her, hungrily exploring his mouth with her own, meeting him move for move, touch for touch. Communicating without words.

Charles ran his fingertips across her back and down along her hips. Every nerve in Laurel's body sang in response, tingling and trilling and crying for more. A beat pulsed in the pit of her stomach and increased like jungle drums growing nearer.

She wanted him.

She wanted to be with him.

And not just for the night, but forever.

Then his phone rang. Startled, Laurel jumped back, quickly raking a hand across her mouth.

Charles laughed. "It's just the phone."

"You should probably answer that."

"I'd just as soon toss it," he said, reaching for her again.

She wanted to sink into his arms but she needed time to think, to figure out what this meant, and what she was going to do about it. "No, you should get it. What if it's an emergency."

"Everyone I'd worry about is safe under this roof," he said.

She nodded, and smiled. "And I should check on Penny now." The truth was, she wanted nothing more than to be with him, but she felt like she should make sure Penny was happily occupied and not standing outside the door watching them, wondering what it all meant.

He shook his head. "This isn't over," he said, taking the ringing phone out of his pocket.

"I'm counting on that," she said, and gave him a brief smile before leaving the room.

"This better be good," Charles growled into the phone.

"It's important," Brendan Brady responded. "Damned important."

Charles sat down. This was obviously about Laurel. He wasn't sure he was in the mood to hear it, but he knew he had to. "What is it?"

"Laurel Midland," Brady began.

A bad feeling crossed Charles's chest. "What about her?"

"She's dead," Brendan Brady said simply. "Laurel Midland is dead."

CHAPTER SIXTEEN

SATISFIED THAT PENNY was absorbed in her movie, Laurel went back to the kitchen feeling like she was walking on air. Before her lay the delicious promise of Charles Gray's kisses, his embrace, and maybe—*maybe*—an actual future with him.

Two months ago she never would have believed that such a thing was possible. Love was as far out of her reach as winning the lottery.

Yet suddenly she felt as if she *had* won the lottery.

And it was a better prize than she could ever have imagined.

When she got back to the kitchen, Charles was sitting on a stool, his phone lying on the counter next to him.

His face was pale, and his expression was that of someone who had just received very bad news.

"Is everything all right?" Laurel asked, knowing the answer was *no* but having no idea what was wrong.

He raised his eyes to her, and for the first time since she'd met him, they were narrowed, and cold, and hard.

"Charles, what's wrong?" she asked, her heart skipping a beat or two.

"You tell me."

"I don't know! Was your phone call bad news?"

He gave a half nod. "You could say that. In fact, you could say it was *very* bad news."

She went to him and put a hand on his shoulder. "What is it? Maybe I can help."

He shrugged her hand off and, finally, she realized it was about her. "I don't think you can."

Her mind raced with possibilities, but she had no idea which terrible scenario had played itself. "Please tell me what's going on," she said, her voice shaking.

"Funny, I was going to say the same thing to you."

"Charles, I don't understand what you're getting at." Her dreams, the happiness and optimism she had felt just moments before, floated up and away, like smoke.

She knew everything had changed, she just wasn't sure why, or what had changed it.

"Why don't you begin," he said coolly, "by telling me who you really are."

She felt the blood leave her face. "Who called you?"

"That was a private investigator I use sometimes on the phone. He did a preliminary background check on you, purely routine, but this afternoon he found out something very disturbing about you."

"What?"

He shook his head. "You answer my questions first, then I'll answer yours. Who are you?"

"My name is Laurel."

"Laurel Midland is dead. She died in a car bomb explosion in Lenovia a month and a half ago."

"I'm Laurel Standish."

"Laurel Standish." He frowned for a moment, then understanding came into his eyes. "The one they thought was in the accident?"

"Yes." Hysteria rose in her breast. Who had he talked to? Who knew the truth?

He looked skeptical. Then, quickly, angry. "I find it hard to believe that all the people you worked with thought you died and didn't wonder where Laurel Midland was the next day. Did they all suddenly go blind and not realize who you were?"

"They knew exactly who I was," Laurel said.

"They protected me by announcing that I was dead. It was my director's idea that I take on Laurel Midland's name so I could get a fresh, safe, start in the States."

He appeared to think about it for a moment, then said, "I don't know if I can believe anything you say."

"Everything I told you about myself, everything I told you about my experience in Lenovia, was true," she went on, her voice strong even though inside she felt like Jell-O.

"Given that the *name* you gave me wasn't true, I find it hard to believe any of it."

She sighed. "I understand that, but if you'll just listen to me, I can explain."

He looked at his watch. "You've got five minutes. Go."

She took a deep, steadying breath, and began. "Laurel Midland and I went to Lenovia together, as part of the American Help Corps. organization. We taught English there together. It was actually a pretty quiet, uneventful life until I realized that drug lords were using local children for drug runs. They'd offer them what amounted to a buck or two, and maybe a handful of candy, to carry drugs across the border. If they got caught or—as was more often the case—shot by rival drug lords and robbed, these guys didn't care. They'd just kick the corpse aside and send the next kid."

Charles still looked skeptical, but something else had entered his expression now as well. Compassion. "Did you let the authorities know about this?"

Laurel scoffed. "Most of the authorities were on the payroll." She shook her head. "There was hardly anyone willing to help, although, yes, I did speak with the authorities. I think that's what put a big bullseye on my back."

He nodded. "Go on."

"Laurel was my best friend there. I told her what I'd discovered and she wanted to help but I didn't want her to be in danger too. It's ironic, now when I look back on it. But I really tried to do the right thing." Tears burned in Laurel's eyes, remembering this thing she hadn't wanted to think about for months now.

Charles's expression had definitely softened. "So what happened?"

"I was supposed to do a supply run one night. Once a week we'd go get food, medicine, soap, that kind of thing from a neighboring town. I always went because I spoke the language better than anyone else in our camp. But on the night…" Her voice trailed off.

"Go on," Charles urged.

She had to tell him the truth. If he still wanted to be angry, or even if he wanted nothing to do with her, then it was out of her control, but at this point she had to tell him the whole truth. No matter how painful it was to recall. "That night I was sick. I had a stomach flu or something. It wasn't a big deal at all, by the next morning I was fine. But, of course, by the next morning, Laurel was dead."

"They bombed her car, thinking she was you."

Tears spilled out over Laurel's cheeks. "I think so." She broke down, crying. "I don't know if it was right or wrong, but my director, my friends, everyone told me to run. They said they'd say it was me in the accident and that Laurel Midland was so upset she went home. Since she didn't have any family left who needed to know one way or the other, it seemed like it could work." She took a long, shuddering breath. "And now that I've said it out loud, it seems more heinous than ever, but now you know the truth."

"And you're safe."

"For what it's worth."

He moved toward her. "It's worth a lot," he said, touching his hand to her cheek. "I'm very glad you're here and you're safe."

She couldn't believe her ears. "You're...*glad?*"

"Of course. Thank goodness your friends protected your identity. Or at least most of them did. My investigator tracked down someone who came back shortly after you did and wanted some quick cash. He told Brady that you weren't the one in the accident."

The betrayal stung bitterly. "What would one of my friends—"

Charles held up a hand. "Brady told him Laurel Standish had an inheritance and he wanted to find her closest relative. The guy probably thought he was doing you a favor."

Laurel swallowed the lump in her throat. She shouldn't have expected anyone to keep such a crazy secret at all. The whole idea had been nuts...she never should have gone along with it. "It's best that it's out in the open now. I felt lost trying to be someone else." She gave a dry laugh. "I'm still lost, but at least now I'm honest."

"You're not lost," Charles said firmly. "You're *found.* You ended up exactly where you belong, here with me. I can't fault any plan that led you here."

Her heart quickened. "You can forgive me?"

"Forgive you? I'd have to be an arrogant ass to think it was my place to forgive you for saving your own life." He looked at her intently. "But I admire you more than I have ever admired anyone." He shook his head. "It's just like you to risk your welfare for that of the children. I just wish you could have told me the truth before." He shook his head. "But I understand why you didn't feel like you could. I don't know how you trust anyone."

She sank against him, languishing in the safety of his warmth. "Oh, Charles…"

"And I promise I'll never let anything happen to you," he went on.

"In fact, I'll have my lawyer get in touch with the state department right away in order to get those thugs in Lenovia taken care of. They are no threat to you," he said fiercely. "Or to anyone else. Never again."

She looked into his eyes and for perhaps the first time in her life she said exactly what was in her heart. She didn't hold back because of fear, or embarrassment, or anything else. "I don't know what I would have done if I hadn't met you. But it felt so wrong to lie. The guilt was overwhelming."

He ran his thumb along her jaw and she leaned against the warmth of his touch. He made her feel so safe.

"No sense in thinking about it," he said, taking her into his arms. "Guilt is a terrible thing to live with. I spent a long time feeling responsible for what happened to Angelina until I finally realized that you can't take responsibility for fate."

"How long did it take you to realize that?"

"Oh, I realized it about a month ago," he said, kissing the top of her head. "When I started to fall in love with you."

She drew back and looked into his eyes. "Fall in love?"

He nodded. "As crazy as it probably sounds, I've fallen in love with you."

She breathed out and sank into him. He was in love with her! "But why?"

"Why?" He laughed. "Why does the sun rise every morning? It's just what happens. It's inevitable. It's meant to be."

"I know what you mean," she said, drawing back and looking into his eyes. "Because I've fallen for you, too."

He smiled, a wide, unguarded smile. "Is that so?"

She smiled too. "Yes, that's so. I love you. You're impossible, but I love you."

"You *do?*" a small voice gasped from the doorway. "You love my daddy?"

They turned to see Penny standing there, hair mussed from sleep, but her eyes wide open and alert. She was smiling as big as her doll Marigold's painted smile.

"Yes, I do," Laurel said with a laugh.

"Which is lucky because your daddy loves her too." He held out his arm and Penny ran into it, as naturally as if they did that all the time. "And I love you, little one."

"I know that!" Penny laughed. "So are you two going to get married? Was the gypsy right after all?"

Laurel and Charles exchanged glances and smiled.

"I guess she was," Charles said. "As hard as it is to believe."

"Oh, *I* believed it the whole time," Penny said, settling herself comfortably between Laurel and Charles. "I told Marigold about it and *she* said you were going to fall in love and get married and live happily ever after." Penny stopped and frowned. "So what do we do next?"

Charles looked from her to Laurel. "What do *you* think we should do next?"

She gave a laugh. "I think we should celebrate Thanksgiving, what do you think?"

"Absolutely." He gave Penny a squeeze and leaned over to give Laurel a kiss and a promise of what was to come. "I've never had more to be thankful for in my life."

EPILOGUE

CHARLES AND LAUREL HAD a long time to talk Thanksgiving night, as the wind blew the snow in ferocious patterns outside. He told her what little Brendan Brady had learned about Laurel and she filled in the rest of the blanks.

However, the one thing she hadn't known before was about having two sisters. As soon as Charles realized she was interested in pursuing her roots, he put his man on the case to try and find someone associated with the now-defunct Barrie Home for Children.

Laurel had tried, too. She'd spent long hours on the internet, registering on sites for people looking for biological parents and siblings, and for biological parents looking for the children they gave up for adoption. But there was nothing.

If Laurel had sisters, if that was really true, then

either they didn't know about her or they didn't care to find her. As time passed, Laurel's optimism that she would find the answers began to wane.

Until one morning about a week after Thanksgiving.

The doorbell rang early in the morning. When Laurel opened it and saw the two women standing there, one blonde, and one redhead, she knew immediately—deep down—that she knew them.

"Yes?"

The two looked at each other, and the blonde spoke. "Are you Laurel Midland?"

"I—" She was confused. She decided to play it close to the vest until she figured out why *anyone* would be asking for her. "I'm Laurel."

It was the blonde who spoke, while the redhead looked on anxiously. "Well, this might seem strange but we know you just got back from working in Lenovia and, actually, we wanted to talk to you about one of your co-workers."

"Who?"

"Laurel Standish."

"Who are you?" Laurel asked, excitement rising in her chest. Could it be? Could it really be?

Was it even *possible?*

"We're her sisters," the redhead said. "I'm Rose,

and this is Lily. We know you haven't heard of us since she didn't know about us, but…" She stopped.

Laurel was crying. She nodded and tried to find her voice.

"I'm sorry if this is painful for you," Lily said, looking uncertainly at her sister. "You see, we only just found out about her. Just a little too late. We know about…about her accident."

And then Rose was crying too.

"I'm Laurel," Laurel managed to say, though the three of them looked so much alike—apart from their hair colors—that it felt like she was stating the obvious. "There was…" She would explain it all later. "There was a mix-up with the accident in Lenovia. I'm," she almost couldn't believe she could say it, "I'm Laurel Standish."

Lily gasped.

Rose went pale. "Laurel?"

Laurel nodded, unable to speak.

"You're really you?" Lily asked, then laughed. "I mean, you're really Laurel Standish? Adopted from the Barrie Home in Brooklyn twenty-six years ago?"

Laurel nodded. "Yes. Yes, that's me. I can't believe this. I—I just found out about you. I've spent a week looking up everything I could to try and find you."

"We didn't even *know* about you until a few weeks ago," Rose said. "And then it was only to hear that you'd...died." She took a short breath. "Are you *really* you?"

Laurel nodded. "I am."

Lily smiled. "I can't believe this. But let's make this formal. I'm your sister Lily, and from what I understand, I'm the oldest. This is Rose, the middle child. And this," she touched Rose's flat stomach, "is your future niece or nephew."

Laurel laughed. "I don't know how much more I can take! Last week I had only my father and today..." She looked at them and blinked back tears. "All of you." It was only then that she realized they were still standing on the front porch. "What am I thinking? Come *in.* We have a *lot* of catching up to do."

"Twenty-six years' worth," Rose agreed.

"Plus or minus a few days," Lily said, walking between the two and taking their hands in hers. "I hope you have some time," she added.

"I've got all the time in the world," Laurel said. "Starting now."

1006 Gen Std HB

NOVEMBER 2006 HARDBACK TITLES

ROMANCE™

The Italian's Future Bride	*Michelle Reid*	0 263 19262 8
Pleasured in the Billionaire's Bed	*Miranda Lee*	0 263 19263 6
Blackmailed by Diamonds, Bound by Marriage	*Sarah Morgan*	0 263 19264 4
The Greek Boss's Bride	*Chantelle Shaw*	0 263 19265 2
The Millionaire's Pregnant Wife	*Sandra Field*	0 263 19266 0
The Greek's Convenient Mistress	*Annie West*	0 263 19267 9
Chosen as the Frenchman's Bride	*Abby Green*	0 263 19268 7
The Italian Billionaire's Virgin	*Christina Hollis*	0 263 19269 5
Outback Man Seeks Wife	*Margaret Way*	0 263 19270 9
The Nanny and the Sheikh	*Barbara McMahon*	0 263 19271 7
The Businessman's Bride	*Jackie Braun*	0 263 19272 5
Meant-To-Be Mother	*Ally Blake*	0 263 19273 3
Falling for the Frenchman	*Claire Baxter*	0 263 19274 1
In Her Boss's Arms	*Elizabeth Harbison*	0 263 19275 X
In Her Boss's Special Care	*Melanie Milburne*	0 263 19276 8
The Surgeon's Courageous Bride	*Lucy Clark*	0 263 19277 6

HISTORICAL ROMANCE™

Not Quite a Lady	*Louise Allen*	0 263 19060 9
The Defiant Debutante	*Helen Dickson*	0 263 19061 7
A Noble Captive	*Michelle Styles*	0 263 19062 5

MEDICAL ROMANCE™

The Surgeon's Miracle Baby	*Carol Marinelli*	0 263 19098 6
A Consultant Claims His Bride	*Maggie Kingsley*	0 263 19099 4
The Woman He's Been Waiting For	*Jennifer Taylor*	0 263 19517 1
The Village Doctor's Marriage	*Abigail Gordon*	0 263 19518 X

1006 Gen Std LP

NOVEMBER 2006 LARGE PRINT TITLES

ROMANCE™

The Secret Baby Revenge	*Emma Darcy*	0 263 19014 5
The Prince's Virgin Wife	*Lucy Monroe*	0 263 19015 3
Taken for His Pleasure	*Carol Marinelli*	0 263 19016 1
At the Greek Tycoon's Bidding	*Cathy Williams*	0 263 19017 X
The Heir's Chosen Bride	*Marion Lennox*	0 263 19018 8
The Millionaire's Cinderella Wife	*Lilian Darcy*	0 263 19019 6
Their Unfinished Business	*Jackie Braun*	0 263 19020 X
The Tycoon's Proposal	*Leigh Michaels*	0 263 19021 8

HISTORICAL ROMANCE™

The Viscount's Betrothal	*Louise Allen*	0 263 18919 8
Reforming the Rake	*Sarah Elliott*	0 263 18920 1
Lord Greville's Captive	*Nicola Cornick*	0 263 19076 5

MEDICAL ROMANCE™

His Honourable Surgeon	*Kate Hardy*	0 263 18891 4
Pregnant with His Child	*Lilian Darcy*	0 263 18892 2
The Consultant's Adopted Son	*Jennifer Taylor*	0 263 18893 0
Her Longed-For Family	*Josie Metcalfe*	0 263 18894 9
Mission: Mountain Rescue	*Amy Andrews*	0 263 19527 9
The Good Father	*Maggie Kingsley*	0 263 19528 7

1106 Gen Std HB

DECEMBER 2006 HARDBACK TITLES

ROMANCE™

Taken by the Sheikh *Penny Jordan*	0 263 19278 4
The Greek's Virgin *Trish Morey*	0 263 19279 2
The Forced Bride *Sara Craven*	0 263 19280 6
Bedded and Wedded for Revenge *Melanie Milburne*	0 263 19281 4
The Italian Boss's Secretary Mistress *Cathy Williams*	0 263 19282 2
The Kouvaris Marriage *Diana Hamilton*	0 263 19283 0
The Santorini Bride *Anne McAllister*	0 263 19284 9
Pregnant by the Millionaire *Carole Mortimer*	0 263 19285 7
Rancher and Protector *Judy Christenberry*	0 263 19286 5
The Valentine Bride *Liz Fielding*	0 263 19287 3
One Summer in Italy... *Lucy Gordon*	0 263 19288 1
Crowned: An Ordinary Girl *Natasha Oakley*	0 263 19289 X
The Boss's Pregnancy Proposal *Raye Morgan*	0 263 19290 3
Outback Baby Miracle *Melissa James*	0 263 19291 1
A Wife and Child To Cherish *Caroline Anderson*	0 263 19292 X
The Spanish Doctor's Convenient Bride *Meredith Webber*	0 263 19293 8

HISTORICAL ROMANCE™

The Wanton Bride *Mary Brendan*	0 263 19063 3
A Scandalous Mistress *Juliet Landon*	0 263 19064 1
A Wealthy Widow *Anne Herries*	0 263 19065 X

MEDICAL ROMANCE™

The Surgeon's Family Miracle *Marion Lennox*	0 263 19100 1
A Family to Come Home to *Josie Metcalfe*	0 263 19101 X
The London Consultant's Rescue *Joanna Neil*	0 263 19519 8
The Doctor's Baby Surprise *Gill Sanderson*	0 263 19520 1

1106 Gen Std LP

DECEMBER 2006 LARGE PRINT TITLES

ROMANCE™

Love-Slave to the Sheikh *Miranda Lee*	0 263 19022 6
His Royal Love-Child *Lucy Monroe*	0 263 19023 4
The Ranieri Bride *Michelle Reid*	0 263 19024 2
The Italian's Blackmailed Mistress *Jacqueline Baird*	0 263 19025 0
Having the Frenchman's Baby *Rebecca Winters*	0 263 19026 9
Found: His Family *Nicola Marsh*	0 263 19027 7
Saying Yes to the Boss *Jackie Braun*	0 263 19028 5
Coming Home to the Cowboy *Patricia Thayer*	0 263 19029 3

HISTORICAL ROMANCE™

An Unusual Bequest *Mary Nichols*	0 263 18921 X
The Courtesan's Courtship *Gail Ranstrom*	0 263 18922 8
Ashblane's Lady *Sophia James*	0 263 19077 3

MEDICAL ROMANCE™

Maternal Instinct *Caroline Anderson*	0 263 18895 7
The Doctor's Marriage Wish *Meredith Webber*	0 263 18896 5
The Doctor's Proposal *Marion Lennox*	0 263 18897 3
The Surgeon's Perfect Match *Alison Roberts*	0 263 18898 1
The Consultant's Homecoming *Laura Iding*	0 263 19529 5
A Country Practice *Abigail Gordon*	0 263 19530 9